RUCKUS

SEAL TEAM ALPHA

ZOE DAWSON

BLUE
MOON
CREATIVE
LLC

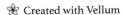

ACKNOWLEDGMENTS

I'd like to thank my beta readers and editor for helping with this book. As always, you guys are the best.

For anyone who has found forgiveness difficult. I hope you find your way.

*Hell, there are no rules here. We are trying to accomplish
something.*

Thomas Edison

1

Darién Gap, Colombia, South America

She woke to the *crack* of gunfire, screaming, and running feet. Before she could move, a gun was shoved into her back. She looked over her shoulder at the merciless dark eyes of the man holding the weapon. "Hello, Dana Sorenson. I've got a job for you."

She'd had a job, one that hadn't turned out as she'd hoped.

Had it only been a week ago she'd been standing on a dock in Turbo, Colombia, a disreputable port town rife with violence on the coast of Colombia and in the horseshoe of the Gulf of Urabá to fulfill her mom's wish. It was just before dawn, the sun nothing but a glimmer on the horizon. She'd waited for a boat that would take her and her crew into the Darién Gap, a place that was teeming with dense jungle, dangerous wildlife, impenetrable swamps, wary guerrillas, intense paramilitary, deadly drug traffickers, disreputable guides and no marked trails.

The Darién might be a ten-thousand-mile swath of inhospitable land, but Dana was a correspondent who, due to her parents' noble example, had given up reporting about the war in exchange for pieces on the human condition. She was now a writer, photographer, filmmaker and contributing editor to *International Humanitarian Journal*. From her war correspondent experience, she could handle stressful encounters and dangerous people as situations that were all in a day's work. She'd had some harrowing experiences in her life but had gotten the story every time. This piece was timely, a hot button, and would allow her to showcase what people would do for freedom and a better life along with keeping her promise to her mom. But going into the Gap had been risky. She'd been well aware of the dangers but had never let that stop her before. These stories needed to be told.

She needed to tell them.

There were several people with her from her film company, along with porters heading to Domingodó to meet up with a representative from the Revolutionary Armed Forces of Colombia, or FARC, Cuba-backed guerrillas who had been at war with Colombia since 1964. They controlled the most direct route through the Gap, and it had been her best chance of meeting and talking to migrants attempting the crossing. Permission had been obtained from an official in Havana to pave the way for her and her crew to do this timely story.

The soft drone of an outboard motor broke the predawn quiet. James Quinn, a freelance videographer she'd hired to document the trip, leaned over and said, "Are you ready for this?"

She smiled. "I was born ready." He and her South African producer and naturalized American, Liam Nelson, were the two crew members accompanying her on the trip. Her cell chimed, and she pulled it out of her cargo pants and read the screen. *Jeffrey*. He had been calling ever since she'd left San Diego and her office to make this trip. She hit the accept button and said, "Hi, there."

"Dana, geez woman, you've been a hard one to get a hold of. I really needed to talk to you before you left. It was important."

"I know, but the okays came through for this trip and I had to go. You understand."

He sighed heavily. "I do. I know how much your mom meant to you." At his words, her eyes filled, and she worked at not losing it. "Look I'd be the first one to say what you do is great. You have more courage than some men I know. I would never stand in the way of that, but—"

"I know, and I promise to make time when I get home." She wiped her slick palm on her pants. Why was this simple conversation with Jeff making her palms sweat? She swallowed and kept her voice nonchalant. Because she had been sure that he was going to pop the question. That's what he wanted to talk to her about—getting married. She wasn't sure she was ready for that. If she would ever be ready for that.

She squeezed her eyes closed on that thought, the unnamed emotion clogging her chest. Every time she thought about marriage, it would crop up like some kind of plague. She'd been in some pretty scary situations, so why did marriage make her want to run for the hills like a scared little girl?

"Promise?" he said.

"Promise," she replied. Dana disconnected the call as the motor boat pulled up beside the dock along with another boat whose engine had been drowned out by their transportation. It was a ferry to Sapzurro and Capurganá where migrants could then traverse overland to La Miel, Panama.

These migrants weren't forced to go through the Gap as they had documentation that would allow them to pass without a problem. That wasn't the route of her story. As her crew loaded up their gear into the motor boat, she'd worry about Jeff when she got home. She didn't need distractions on this trip.

People without documentation were forced to hire coyotes, part of the *Clan Los Piratas* who would charge between five hundred to seven hundred dollars and transport them in poorly maintained boats, often leaking. But were also notorious for conscripting migrants as mules, then disposing of them.

That had been her story.

Clan Los Piratas was a neo-paramilitary group with upwards of twenty thousand members and the most dangerous group in the area. Dana had read that they had murdered several Americans, many DEA agents and were on the US government's list. They had a stronghold in the Darién Gap, but she was confident they wouldn't bother them with their FARC approval and their sanctioned story about the migrants. She had to wonder if she'd been totally wrong.

Even as the sun rose, and the misty jungle lay like a dense, dark giant across the river, she shivered in the steamy air. The man who had was threatening her had the steely look of one who was used to being in control.

Heading into the world's most dangerous jungle hadn't been on Dana Sorensen's radar until months ago when she'd gotten an email from her dying mother asking Dana to do something for her. *Tell these peoples' stories. Let the public know what was happening.* It had been the last correspondence Dana had received before her mom—her brave, beautiful, accomplished mom—had lost her fight with cancer.

As a surgeon involved with Doctors Without Borders, her mom had met and married Dana's dad, who was a nurse also serving with them. She often wondered if she could even live up to her mom's ability to be so selfless.

Even as the tears moistened her eyes, Dana tried to tell herself that she had no way of knowing her mom was going to go so fast, before Dana could get home. And with guilt pressing in from all sides, eating at her, the grief still fresh, Dana was going to fulfill her mom's dying wish. Come hell or high water.

She'd pitched her mom's story to the editor for *Trek Magazine* about migrants travelling through the Darién Gap to make it from Colombia to Panama, then up through the Central American peninsula with the final destination the US. It had all stemmed out of her mom's last trip to Asia where she'd found out that a lot of migrants were heading through South America to bypass the routes that had dried up due to stronger restrictions. And it wasn't just Asia, but a slew of foreigners looking for a better life free from war and persecution.

After meeting their contact, Captain Enrique Escobar, a middle-aged, dark-haired man with gray at the temples and in his close-cropped beard, his sharp eyes and features telling Dana he had seen plenty in the Gap, they were transported into the Gap. During the past dire week, with the constant threat of robbery, kidnapping, and death, he and his men hiked the route, while she and her crew recorded one of the world's most dangerous journeys. She and her crew hacked through spider-infested mangrove swamps, walking for days in muggy, ninety-degree temperatures, the migrants surviving on crackers and gulping river water. Each of these people—a man from Jafar, Bangladesh trying to escape its cutthroat political gangs and miserable working conditions; another Bangladesh woman, not much more than a girl; a rural laborer who'd gone to the jam-packed cities for work and found herself locked in the bowels of unlicensed garment factories working for twenty cents an hour; and countless others, Syrians, West Africans, and Cubans—had made the terrible trek with them. She'd interviewed many of them who told their heartbreaking stories.

She and her crew had documented everything on memory cards, and they were carefully kept in a waterproof bag in her pack. By accident, she found some old footage of her and her mom when she'd met up with her overseas and interviewed her for a piece that had never been aired. Stupidly, she'd forgotten about it and realized this was her only copy. She'd edit this and get it aired when she got home. She'd contact someone she knew at *60 Minutes* or *National Geographic* who would jump at the chance.

But once they had reached their destination, they had been stopped by Senafront, Panamanian soldiers who'd guarded the border; the travelers' hopes of freedom and respite had been dashed. The migrants had been denied entry into Panama, and everything they had suffered and endured had been in vain. Fighting her sense of justice, she tried to tell the Panamanian patrol what kind of journey they had made, how courageous they had been. The officer was sympathetic, but he had no choice—he had to follow orders.

There was nothing she could do. All that had been left for her was to tell their story, document their journey so that their efforts meant something. A painful discomfort under her sternum along with a healthy dose of guilt suffused her as she'd boarded a *piragua* to take them to Panama City and the airport for their trip out of the Gap. Home to San Diego to civilization, concrete and glass, teeming with urbanites. But her uneasiness hadn't gone away. She'd tried to think about processing the film and documenting the trip. Her heart was heavy with real sorrow for the plight of the people she'd gotten to know so well in the week of traveling with them through the dangerous and deadly Gap and an emptiness deep inside she couldn't name for fear of...what?

As a storm came up quickly and violently out of the south, they were forced to pull to the bank to wait it out.

Dana had pitched her waterproof tent and settled inside, lying down on her side. As the leaded sky had darkened, she'd fallen into a fitful sleep.

Now she had been hustled out of her warm, dry tent, her hands up and there was a gun on her.

"Who are you?" she demanded. "What do you want?"

"Oh, before too long you will know who I am and what I want."

A black hood descended, cutting off light and hope. When she fought, someone clipped her on the back of the head and she fell to the ground.

She'd been taken.

Kidnapped.

~

SOMEWHERE OVER MEXICO

Lieutenant Bowie "Ruckus" Cooper leaned his head against the side of the chopper. He could sleep anywhere and often had in his twenty years in the SEALs. They had just lifted up from Mexico in support of the DEA and their operations. With a high-value target, or HVT, secured, they were headed back to Coronado and some R&R.

Seven other SEALs were in the chopper with him. Part of his deployment team, his family, his brothers. They were all cut from the same cloth, and there was comfort in that, a unity among them that was unique and recognized between them. Normally, SEALs deployed in either eight-man squads or four-man teams.

The men he trained and fought with built close personal bonds between them. Probably the most important part of a team was the utmost trust they had for each other. It saved Ruckus when the inconsistency and heartache of his family situation left him alone at seventeen.

Each SEAL's control over his thinking was what separated them from everyone else.

Right across from him was Ruckus's point man and lead sniper, Petty Officer Ashe "Kid Chaos" Wilder. A man who lived up to his name. Never reckless, often a smart-ass, but always courageous, Kid was the youngest member of their team and one of the best shots in the navy.

Next to him was Chief Petty Officer Wes "Cowboy" McGraw, an honest to God cowboy from Texas who had lived and manned a working ranch, from the kind of stock that tamed the Old West and were recruited as Texas Rangers. He attained his rank in record time and wore his anchor, the symbol of his rank and that of the navy, with the kind of honor it embodied. Navy chiefs kept tradition, ceremony, and honor alive—a true anchor of the navy. He was Ruckus's valued go-to second when things got hairy and his main planning buddy.

To his right was Petty Officer Thorn "Tank" Hunt, their K9 handler who could juggle combat and a weapon with ease, and his dog Echo, a Belgian Malinois who reclined right next to him, quiet and alert. He was an exacting guy not only with everyone he met, but with himself, a tough taskmaster who took "control freak" to a new level. The man could commandeer, drive, pilot, navigate, or ride anything with wheels or runners.

To Cowboy's left was Petty Officer Ocean "Blue" Beckett, a fair-haired California surfer dude that could outswim anyone in Team Seven. He was their sniper and expert corpsman, so skilled the guy could've become a doctor if he hadn't decided on the SEALs as his career. He was a boy-next-door type on steroids, loved that touchy/feely crap but could balance it with his fierce warrior instincts and a Yoda/Obi-Wan Kenobi, Jedi master/sage philosopher attitude who would often stun them with his insights.

Then came their communication expert and air controller, Petty Officer Arlo "Scarecrow" Porter, a Southern badass from bayou country who knew how to charm everyone but excelled specifically with the fairer sex. He was affable until you put him in a firefight and watched him go to town. He was adept at bringing attack aircraft to the exact coordinates when they needed them for egress or cover and a true orator with Tom Sawyer skills of manipulation.

Petty Officer Orion "Wicked" Cross, a tall, quiet gourmet cook, and master of detail sat next to Scarecrow. Wicked was limitless, an Olympic-level rower before BUD/S and the team's breacher, sniper, and lead assaulter. Typical of the men here, he didn't like being told what to do, but then these men were dedicated to the team and getting the job done. It was all about giving Wicked as much rope as possible to do his thing while staying on point both in the military and in combat.

Finally, there was Petty Officer Jude "Hollywood" Lock, their heavy weapons expert. He had to be the most positive guy Ruckus had ever met and knew all about entertainment, in any context—board games, cards, sports, movies, and even Broadway, the guy was a master. He smiled no matter the climate or condition, a definite boost in any group. Ruckus was sure the guy would explode if he couldn't help someone, somewhere, at all times. Sometimes Ruckus thought his actual nickname should have been Boy Scout. He would definitely drop everything to usher an old lady across the street. He was also the team's most notorious lothario.

Just as he was drifting off, his headset came alive.

"Lieutenant Cooper?"

"Cooper here," Ruckus said keying his mic, his head coming off the glass, instantly alert.

"Change of plans." It was the voice of his mentor and task unit commander, Major Todd McRae.

Ruckus smiled. That's what this job was all about.

The next thing he knew they were landing on the USS *Annenberg*, out of Naval Base Coronado, an aircraft supercarrier named after Admiral Jake "Tugboat" Annenberg. The carrier floated just off the coast of Panama, a warship that served as an airbase with a flight deck and home to thirty-two hundred sailors and marines and twenty-four hundred aviators. All eight of them and Echo exited the aircraft, still looking worse for wear. They crossed the flight deck to a waiting figure.

"Lieutenant Cooper," Major Todd McRae said, and he nodded to Ruckus and the men behind him. He shook Ruckus's hand. "We're aware you guys have been in the field, but we've got a HVT we need you to go after. We just got the intel and you were the closest and best match. First, let's get you some chow." Tall, his dark hair going to salt and pepper, Todd had been with Ruckus through his formative years with the navy, directed him into officer training and been the father Ruckus had needed.

"Aye, sir," Ruckus said as they headed to the mess and ate their fill, cleaned up as much as they could, and restocked both their ammo and field kits for a three-day LRRP, a long-range reconnaissance patrol.

Once that was complete, they headed up to a ready room complete with comfortable chairs.

When McRae walked in, Ruckus said, "Attention on deck!"

Everyone rose until McRae said, "As you were, gentlemen."

Returning to their seats, the major turned off the lights, and an illuminated map of the Darién Gap appeared. He walked to the head of the room and said, "For those of you who haven't ever had the pleasure of being deployed into the Darién Gap, you're in for a treat. It's a thick jungle with mostly crude villages, para-military, FARC, and clans fighting over freedom, drugs, and routes. Be aware there are civilians in this area, some hikers, missionaries, and, of course, the peaceful indigenous population, so use caution when engaging. It's a mishmash of a mess. Deep in the jungle here..." He pointed to an area outlined in red in the heart of the greenery. "...is your target." A picture flashed up on the screen. "This is Hector Salazar, the leader of *Clan Los Piratas*, or the CLP as they're widely known. He is an American by birth, but with a Colombian mother, he had ties to this area. Now he's worked his way up the criminal drug runner's ladder and is the new kingpin. He's taken disenfranchised former para-military members from splinter groups and built an empire that is now warring with anyone in the Gap for control. The competition for massive drug profits is fierce and with the recent peace accords, it's left a vacuum to fill."

"His mom must be so proud," Kid said, and the guys laughed.

Ruckus studied the picture of Salazar. He looked more like a billionaire playboy than a drug runner in an open collar shirt and white jacket, tanned, of medium height with a honed body and a face that would turn female heads, but the light in his eyes would definitely turn off many of the savvier women. He had a full head of black hair he wore swept back in a style that suggested vanity.

"He is responsible for the deaths of six DEA agents and several American missionaries. The attorney general wants him in the States to stand trial for his crimes. We want him extracted alive."

"If it's not possible," Kid piped up, "we take him out?"

"Affirmative," McRae said.

Either way, justice will be served," Cowboy said in his deep voice.

"This is Angel Nunez, his second-in-command." A second picture flashed onto the screen. Nunez was a different animal altogether, and Angel was definitely a misnomer. His head was ruthlessly shaved; glittering black eyes and a vicious look around his mouth warned of the kind of violence that showed no mercy. The man had some hard-packed muscle and was probably about six two. He was dressed in camo, and Ruckus suspected, out of the two of them, Nunez was more dangerous.

"Intel says that he's not at the compound," McRae continued. "But in Mexico with their business associates, so he shouldn't be a factor." He turned from the screen and said, "You'll HALO over Yaviza and glide to the drop zone just south of the town. You will consider the situation on the ground as hostile. Make your way to the stronghold and obtain the package. You will be extracted to the west at LZ Foxtrot. Any questions?"

"We're under the radar on this one, sir?" Blue asked.

"Copy that, it's black. Avoid any direct action with the natives if possible, but if someone fires on you, defend yourselves. I'm sure Panama won't be too upset to get rid of Salazar, but they'll be pissed to find unsanctioned SEALs on their soil."

The debrief over, they headed to the waiting plane that would take them over the DZ. Thirty minutes later, Ruckus looked around at the camo faces, the paint thick to hide the brightness of their skin. If they were spotted dropping into the jungle, they could easily be shot out of the sky before they landed.

"How you guys holding up?" Ruckus asked.

"Good to go, LT," was the murmured response. Ruckus expected nothing less from his SEALs. Didn't matter that they'd had about four hours sleep in twenty-four. Echo gave him a quick look that said he was ready, too. He was in a harness, belted to Tank's chest, ready to get airborne like the rest of them.

"I'd say pretty boy Blue needs his beauty rest, though," Kid said.

"Kiss my ass," Blue responded in his no-nonsense voice.

"I would if you'd shave it." Kid hooked on his oxygen mask and snapped it in place, his blue eyes dancing in the dim light of the cargo bay.

"Hey, stop picking on Blue. That hair on his ass matches his back," Hollywood quipped, his voice muffled in the mask.

There was laughter all around, and Blue gave them both a double finger salute.

"Approaching DZ. Load up."

They all stood up and approached the bay doors as they lowered in a hydraulic grind, the burst of air pushing them back slightly.

The flight master yelled, "Go."

Kid was the best navigator, and he went out the door first, followed closely by the rest of the team. Using a compass, he would be sight point.

Thirty K up, the temperature was frigid, but warmed as they fell, the ground rushing toward them at one hundred and twenty miles per hour before he saw the first chute open. At the right time, Ruckus deployed his, abruptly slowing his silent descent into a mass of steaming green.

And into hostile territory.

This was the most vulnerable time for a spec ops guy free-floating to a target.

As he dropped lower into the deep valley, the wind yanked at his tight-fitting black jumpsuit, the hot air warming him and slowing his descent. Through his night-vision visor, he saw lights from Yaviza near the winding river. Below him was nothing but a black maw, accelerating toward his face. It was a personal high. He didn't get excited about many things, but jumping out of a speeding aircraft topped the list. That and sex.

He aimed for the sweet spot, a small clearing that would be tough to hit without getting snagged in the dense trees. Kid, Cowboy, Hollywood, and Blue were already down. With Ruckus's boots brushing the treetops, he pulled the suspension lines of the parachute close, rapidly driving him toward the ground.

Touching down with a thump, he tucked and rolled, pulling the black chute with him. He released the oxygen mask, then unhooked his helmet, on one knee, weapon aimed as the remaining SEALs landed in a billow of black nylon.

Being prepared was the best course of action. Switching the visor to thermal, he surveyed his surroundings, sweating inside the suit and his uniform. It showed him nothing but dense forest and a family of monkeys.

Easy in, he thought. Entering the country under the radar kept them invisible for now. In the dark, Ruckus stripped. All of them removed their suits, wrapped their jump gear in the chute, then buried everything.

The team assembled as Ruckus positioned foliage over the pile and dusted his hands. Tank had his GPS out and was marking their route to the stronghold.

They were about ten klicks out—approximately six miles—and would have to hump it to the target area. He didn't expect military checkpoints or patrols, but there could be plenty of *Las Piratas* stalking their territory and protecting their routes. Echo would alert them to anyone in the vicinity.

He adjusted his tech vest filled with gear and ammo, in addition to the rucksack he swung to his back. Tank was checking Echo's harness, a high-tech vest, and proceeded to the head of the line. Behind him, the guys broke their defensive perimeter position to line up behind Tank, all of them careful to maintain their spacing discipline.

Though the monkeys were already screaming warnings to each other, he wanted to get in, do the job, obtain the package, and get out with everyone still breathing.

There was no doubt in his mind that would be the outcome. Positive thinking was the road to success. He'd memorized the terrain, but he'd been in enough jungles to know his way around dense undergrowth. Yet, in the dark, he would rely on Tank and his glowing GPS. The moon was just cresting, and the rain forest was wet, hot and dark.

Echo took the lead, his black snout moving between the ground and the air, loping along. He would alert them to any hidden tangos.

They hacked through the undergrowth, listening for movement and hearing only the squawk of macaws and seeing white-faced monkeys hovering overhead as they worked their way toward the target. Giant kapok and rubber trees shadowed the valley, the ground spread with a gray-white mist that wrapped the giant palms and curled toward the sky, where it hovered, ghost-like in the jungle canopy. The roots smothered the ground so much that his boots rarely touched the soil.

Ruckus ignored the sounds around him, the movement of creatures, the fall of nuts, the scurrying of a green iguana hightailing it into the thicket. He watched as Cowboy checked the compass on his watch. As they neared the stronghold, his gaze moved over the land, searching for any signs of human life.

Nothing.

He gripped his weapon and they all crouched as they came to the edge of a clearing, the stronghold below them. Concrete walls and a huge house sat in the center. There were roving patrols moving silently below them.

"Spread out," Ruckus said, and the SEALs complied. "Tank."

The big SEAL rose, gave Echo a command, and the dog took off with Tank close to him. He would be checking for any explosives.

After a tense few minutes, Tank's voice came over the comm. "Clear, LT. There are two guards at the gate, a barracks to the left, but only three roving patrols. Two guys at the front door."

"Copy," Ruckus said. He turned to the team. "We're going in." He checked his M4. "Kid, neutralize the group to the left. Cowboy, take the right. Hollywood and Wicked, stay here to cover our backs. The rest of you are with me. Keep the noise to a minimum."

"That's five guys," Kid said. "Easy peasy."

"Sure, small potatoes. Didn't you once take out fifteen?" Scarecrow said.

"No," Kid said on a huff of laughter. "I might be bat shit crazy, but I'm not suicidal. It was only fourteen." As the guys laughed, Kid pushed his weapon onto his back, pulled out his tactical knife, crouched low and disappeared. Cowboy did the same, the six-foot five SEAL melting into the night like liquid darkness.

The rest of them slipped down the incline and approached the gates. Kid and Cowboy had already cleared the guards; they were nothing but lumps on the ground. Tank and Echo joined them.

Once inside the walls, Ruckus headed straight for the front door, up the garden path paved with flagstones, flowering bushes and plants along the border. Was this guy for real?

"Hey, Cowboy," Kid whispered. "You think this is some kind of garden party?"

"Shoot, boy. Don't look like it. I don't smell no tea or ladies perfume," he murmured.

Even Ruckus smirked. Cowboy would never live down the garden party incident, and it would forever be a source of ribbing from the guys.

Tank released Echo, and he kept the two guards at the front door busy until Blue took them out with suppressed head shots. The four of them waited until Kid and Cowboy materialized out of the gloom. Blue was already crouched and within seconds had the door open. It swung wide with no noise. Kid's M4 bucked, and the two men who were standing in the hall went down.

"Tank, watch our sixes. Blue, Cowboy, downstairs. Scarecrow, take this floor. Kid, you're with me."

"Copy," came the soft replies.

Ruckus headed up the stairs. The thermal scope told him that there were two tangos on the top floor and five in the basement. When he stealthed up the stairs, he took out the guards and saw the heat signature registering from one of the bedrooms, not the master. He frowned. Where was Salazar?

"Kid."

Without needing any more communication than that, he crouched and picked the lock.

They burst through, but both of them stopped dead. Instead of a hostile, a woman gasped and looked at them, her hand clutched to her throat, startled into a frozen statue. All five feet five of her in practically nothing with tanned legs, dangerous curves, and slick dark hair.

"Damn, LT. She's wearing a towel."

"What was that?" Male voices filled the comm.

"Clear the channel and focus on what you're doing." God help him. All knuckleheads.

Sure enough, the woman was in nothing but baby blue terry cloth in a hot tropical jungle, on a hot tropical night, mean tropical bad guys surrounding the house. Drug thugs were so plentiful you could hit one with a rock, and this honey was smack dab in the middle of it all. If the human filth didn't get her, the wildlife would.

He couldn't take his eyes off the gorgeous brunette, and

it had nothing to do with monitoring her for any type of threat. He swallowed. She had weapons aplenty, the strained terry leaving nothing to the imagination and almost a tad too small for her lithe curves. The law of physics guaranteed that something was going to fall out of that towel, and so help him God, he didn't want to miss anything when it happened.

Her long, thick hair was wet, water still dripping from the dark mass, tendrils stuck to her upper chest and one tantalizing shoulder.

"Who are you?" she said, her voice more firm than breathless.

"I could ask you the same thing."

"You're American?" Those almond-shaped, sultry brown eyes widened, then she blinked in relief.

"Navy SEALs, ma'am," Kid said. Ruckus wasn't the only one to notice her. Kid was young and randy. His eyes caressed her from head to toe.

He nudged the younger SEAL with his shoulder, and Kid gave him an innocent look.

She breathed a sigh. "Thank God. Dana Sorenson. I'm a reporter—"

"Don't move," Ruckus said, all his muscles clenching when she started forward. Saving damsels in distress was in his mission statement and in his job description. If she turned out to be telling the truth, his priority had just changed. Saving anyone, especially an American, was most definitely listed somewhere, but she wasn't the package he was looking for, and he had no idea if she was telling the truth. He wasn't putting himself or his men in jeopardy for this cupcake just yet.

"What? Why? My crew members are being held in the basement. You've got to help them."

"I'm not going to take anything you say at face value, lady. Just stay where you are." Ruckus never took chances until he was one hundred percent sure. They were in a hostile environment and women weren't to be trusted even if they seemed to be exactly what they said they were. This was an unexpected complication.

"Where do you think she has her weapon stashed?" Kid whispered, giving Ruckus a quick, amused glance.

"Kid, go downstairs and help Scarecrow."

"But, LT," Kid whined.

"Go."

"Yes...uh, sir." With a last look at Dana, he turned and slipped down the hall, disappearing down the stairs.

"LT," Cowboy's voice came through his earpiece. "Three tangos down. But there are two guys down here, two American citizens. Worse for wear. One of them is unconscious, the other one says they're journalists."

"Stand by," Ruckus murmured. Her safety and the safety of her crew was utmost in his mind. They were surrounded by killers, and it was apparent her colleagues had been treated poorly and held against their will. That pissed him off and made him doubly determined to get Salazar. Getting them medical attention was imperative, especially for the man that was unconscious.

"We have ID downstairs in Salazar's safe along with my memory cards. What about my crew? Are you going to help them? Are they all right?"

"Get dressed," he ordered, not even lowering the M4 an inch.

Her brows rose at his order. She set her hands on her hips. "Make up your mind. Do you want me to stay put or get dressed?"

"Move and get dressed," he said through clenched teeth.

This woman was going to be a handful of trouble. He immediately got his mind off his hands and her person. She huffed out a breath and bent over—sweet hell—and reached for her clothes on the bed.

She paused and looked up at him. "If you could give me some privacy...."

He didn't answer. His response was clear on his face and in his eyes.

"At least turn around."

"Nope."

"Close your eyes?"

"Just get dressed. Now."

She picked up a pair of black lace panties. Ruckus worked to keep his mind on watching her, not thinking about where that black lace would cover her. She slipped them up her legs and under the towel. She snatched up the pants, muttering under her breath, pulled them on and fastened them. Then she reached for her bra, this time a silky white. She turned around and dropped the towel, revealing the creamy expanse of her back. He felt his body stir as she moved all that long dark hair and fastened the hooks. Then she turned around and picked up her shirt. With angry jerks, she was finally fully clothed. He wasn't sure if he was happy about that.

"Can I use my comb or will you consider that a deadly weapon?"

2

She realized this SEAL was being cautious, and she couldn't blame him for that. It was that she was sick of being ordered around and terrified. Yeah, that had gotten old five minutes after that hood had been jammed over her head.

"Where is Salazar?"

"He's gone."

"Where?"

"I'm not telling you until I see my friends and get my memory cards." She didn't have much to bargain with, and she figured this was going to get her in trouble, but that was nothing new when going after a story. She wasn't leaving this jungle without those cards. They had gone through a lot to get that footage, but it was more than that...her mom's irreplaceable interview. Dana's promise was all tied up in those cards. She wasn't budging on this. The only memory cards that Salazar had let her hold on to were his interviews. One that wasn't finished. But he had other plans and had left about a day ago on urgent business.

The SEAL just gestured with that wicked semi-automatic, looking every inch the badass. His features were hard to make out under that camo paint, with his weapon against his cheek, but those blue eyes of his were steely beneath his dark, frowning brows, and his voice meant business.

She grabbed the comb and pulled it through her hair, quickly braiding it and wrapping an elastic around the end. She threw it behind her when she was done. Then she put everything inside her pack and swung it to her back.

"I'm ready to go. But I'll need to actually walk to get out of this room."

Those hard eyes never even softened. "After you," he said, his voice both deep and menacing.

She hadn't been allowed out of here since she'd tried to escape when Hector Salazar gave her access to the patio. In addition to being an egomaniac, Salazar was a letch. The way he watched her made her skin crawl, but he hadn't touched her. She figured he wanted his interview bad enough that he was willing to wait. She had no illusions that once he got what he wanted, he would take what he had been promising with his dark, glittering eyes.

Talk about feeling powerless and scared. But now with this man at her back, intimidating as hell, she was feeling a lot better, safer.

When she went down the stairs, she saw Liam and James had been liberated from the basement and were in the hall. Liam was propped against the wall and James was prone. She rushed the rest of the way and went to her knees. When she softly touched Liam's face, he opened his eyes. His dazed look made her gut twist. His eyes were tormented, bruises visible on his chin and temple, blood encrusted ligature marks around his wrists and ankles, his lips cracked with healing sores, a sure sign of dehydration. That bastard had told her they were being treated like kings. The lying scum! She had pleaded with Salazar daily to let her crew go, but he wanted them held to make her do as she was told, and it had worked.

"Oh God, Liam. It's so good to see you." She hugged him, and he gently patted her back. There was a bottle in his hand. One of them had gotten him water.

"I'm hanging in there, boss. But James. He tried to fight them. They hit him in the head. He hasn't woken up."

She moved to James and saw that there was a dressing on his forehead and his skin was pale, his body showing the same kind of mistreatment as Liam. One of the SEALs crouched down. His ocean blue eyes were calm and direct, his features arresting with a strong jaw and fine, full lips. "He's in a coma." Those confident, golden-lashed eyes held hers for a considerably long moment. "I couldn't rouse him. We'll get him medical attention as soon as we get you out of here."

Her mouth tightened as her heart caught. She reached out and clasped his forearm. "Coma?" She looked down at James. He really didn't have any family, but she vowed she would make sure he was taken care of. Liam was the one with a wife and child. All this made her feel even worse. Of course, they knew the risks when they agreed to come with her, but that didn't help one bit. Salazar was an animal. "Thank you for taking care of him..."

"Blue, ma'am."

"Blue, thank you."

She looked up at the other hulking bodies, covered in camouflage, bristling with weapons, and was so damn thankful they'd found them. The tallest of them—at least six five, with a pair of thick, sultry lips—had the most intense gaze she'd ever seen, and a face made up of angles instead of curves. Hard-edged. Handsome wasn't the right word for him, but striking fit him to a T.

"This is taking too dang long," he said, his speech slow with a Texas twang. "LT, we need to get them out of here pronto."

"Copy that," Blue said.

She looked over her shoulder and at their "LT." She suspected the moniker was a nickname for lieutenant. He nodded, his eyes losing some of that edge, replaced by anger as he looked to her crew. Maybe he was just being cautious. It was true he didn't know her, and she knew from experience people in desperate situations lied all the time.

The one who had busted into her room, the one called Kid, stood looking out the front door. He nodded. "It's up to LT, Cowboy," Kid said. He looked like a kid, not more than his early twenties, but he was tall and well built, looked barely old enough to shave—let alone carry the assault weapon in his hands, a lethal looking rifle on his back, and a pistol in a holster at his hip.

Sniper, she thought, the word easily describing him. That's what he was in this group. Point man, the lead guy who gathered intel, sniffed out trouble, and took care of that trouble with the business end of his rifle.

Kid looked at the SEAL across from him. "Tank, man, it's too quiet out there," he murmured.

Tank, his vigilance surrounding him like an aura, was built like a tank with impossibly broad shoulders, a black beard, and a pair of intent cinnamon brown eyes. They were constantly on the move as he surveyed the grounds. The dog next to him was beautiful and just as alert as the SEAL. He had a fawn coat and a black mask across his eyes and covering his muzzle. Highly intelligent brown eyes surveyed the grounds.

The titan with a computer to her right looked over at the one they called LT, Mister Charming, who'd refused to even turn around so she could get dressed. She'd never felt so self-conscious in her life. Putting on her unmentionables with a deadly weapon pointed at her was a new experience.

"Ruckus, we're going to have company soon," he said, his voice cultured and so Southern sweet it gave her a toothache. It spoke of the Deep South with lush bayou and long, hot summers. But it was incongruous with all those angles and toughness.

Ruckus? That said it all. He looked like he could cause a few altercations, and not just because of his crazy military skills. Those eyes hadn't been all business. Especially after she'd turned around and saw the way he was looking at her. Unlike Salazar, it made everything in her tingle.

"Copy that, Scarecrow. Up, lady. Let's get your stuff and get moving. The sooner we get your memory cards, the sooner we can bug out of here."

The SEALs all exploded into motion. Blue, the one with the bright blue eyes, the medic, grabbed James and muscled him across his shoulders in a fireman's carry. He rose in one fluid motion while Cowboy picked up Liam and situated him the same way. "You guys start for the LZ. We're right behind you," Ruckus growled.

"Dana," Liam called, concern in his weakened voice.

She gave her friends one more look and said to Liam, "We're getting out of here. I'll be fine," she assured him. Then she hurried to the study. Once inside, she went behind Salazar's desk and crouched down. Removing the floor panel, she made room for the SEAL to see it. "Back up," he barked. Orders seemed to be the extent of his communication skills.

Keeping his eyes on her, he used one hand to take something gray and putty-like from his vest and attach it to the safe. Then he was up, crowding her away from the safe towards the balcony doors. "I'm blowing the safe. When I do, we're going to have company. Keep moving," he said into the mic.

When a small explosion detonated, the desk rattled and a puff of smoke and some fire erupted. He moved swiftly to the safe.

"Copy that," he said grimly. He was obviously talking through his throat mic to his now departing men.

She knelt down and reached into the safe, grabbing a bundle of credentials and then frantically rooted around. "They're not here," she said, her throat getting thick, her chest filling with frustration. "He took them to make sure I followed through. That scum!"

"We've got company, and we're now cut off from our escape route," Ruckus growled.

He rose and grabbed her arm and propelled her to the balcony doors. "No, you keep going. Get those wounded men to the LZ." He none too gently hustled her through the doors. "Don't argue with me, Kid. That's a fucking order." At the railing, she could hear automatic gunfire from the front of the house. He pulled her to the stairs and they rushed down them so fast, she almost stumbled. He dragged her behind him, and before she could even breathe, his gun bucked in his hands. It was loud, louder than she could ever have imagined. Bullets whizzed past. She swore she could feel the heat of one zoom by her cheek.

Suddenly, he turned and pulled her with him. "Run and don't stop until I tell you to."

～

KID RAN with his teammates as automatic gunfire sounded behind them. They were cut off from their leader and that pissed him off. There was no way they were leaving him or the babe behind.

"Cowboy."

"Move, Kid. No time for debate."

"But Ruckus and the reporter."

"He can take care of himself. We have our marching orders. Now move!"

Kid didn't budge. Technically Cowboy outranked him, but he didn't give a damn. "I'm going to lay down some cover. I'll meet you at the chopper."

"Goddammit, Kid. Ruckus will have your head," Cowboy roared to Kid's retreating back.

"I'm going to make sure he has that opportunity," he threw over his shoulder. Kid hooked the strap of his M4 across his chest, pulling the TAC-338 rifle from his back. On the run, he opened his bipod support at the stock of the weapon.

It was child's play to take up a concealed position. He'd already scoped it out as they were moving toward the stronghold. Kid was a master at it whether he was taking enemy fire or he was inserting himself just feet from his targets. He went flat on a small rise above the compound, the bipod keeping the muzzle off the ground. He saw Ruckus and the woman bolt out the back, a solid wall of CLP between them and the LZ, a locked gate and guards in front of them.

He set the stock against his cheek and hugged the earth. Sighting into his scope, he started shooting between heartbeats and breaths to reduce his body movement and give him a more accurate aim, picking them off as he went, going for body shots, letting hydrostatic shock do his work for him. The high velocity round caused damage with the actual penetration, but the shockwave of the round was enough to rupture internal organs and fracture bone.

His suppressive fire gave LT and the babe a fighting chance, caused chaos and even more disorganization. He thought briefly of his dad, in this same situation, the odds stacked against him. If he'd had someone covering his back when he'd been killed in action, Kid wouldn't have grown up without him.

Kid's blood went cold as he saw the fortified gate. There was no way to blow—

An explosion rocked the compound, the concussion killing the men around the area and blowing the gate to smithereens. Kid turned to look up. Hollywood dropped the bazooka from his shoulder, grinning, and said, "*Hoo-yah.* Let's bug out, Chaos, my man."

With Kid's job done, he grabbed the hand Hollywood offered him. Keeping low, they melted into the jungle.

This was only phase one of his plan. There was no way he was leaving Ruckus out there with a civilian.

No way in hell.

He made the LZ just as the chopper was landing. Blue and Cowboy set Dana's two injured crew members inside. Cowboy looked back.

"Ah, you were worried about me," Kid said.

"Get in the damn, chopper, both of you," he said, but it was clear he was relieved to see them. They piled into the chopper, Blue giving Liam additional medical assistance; Scarecrow cradled James Quinn's head in his lap so he wouldn't be lying unconscious on the floor. Buffeted by columns of warm air rising out of the jungle, the chopper motored over a low ridge, signaling the entrance to a dense valley, an endless span of green extending into the cloud-covered peaks of a mountain range.

Ruckus and the pretty reporter were down there running for their lives. But if he had to place odds on who was going to come out of it alive, it would be his LT, hands down.

Cowboy set a hand on his shoulder and Kid turned to him. "As soon as we land, drop these guys off, we're going back."

"You calling the shots, now?" Kid said with a grin. His and Hollywood's actions had not only saved the babe's and their leader's lives but had given Kid a pure adrenaline rush.

WHEN MEN STARTED DROPPING around them, Dana realized they were getting "backup" from Ruckus's team. Her stomach had clenched, her heart racing when she'd spied the gate they were rushing toward. Armed men were firing back. They had been boxed in, the gate locked, then the explosion, a snap of fire, and a starburst of orange flame had ripped through the night, debris flying everywhere, bodies littering the area.

Ruckus said, "*Hoo-yah*, that's the way to do it, guys." Another explosion rocked the ground behind them, shouts of pain and thuds, followed by kicked up rocks and dirt raining down on them. Then there was nothing but the disjointed view of plants and brush, nothing but running into the deep foliage and nothing but the sound of harsh breathing.

Hers.

She had to control her panic. This kind of breathing would only cause her to pass out. She was a runner. She knew how to run and regulate her breaths. They wended through the trees as the sound of crashing bodies spurred her even faster.

He turned to fire several times, gunfire arcing across the perimeter, and she heard cries of pain. He was so impressive the way he worked his weapon and kept moving on those long legs, pulling her with him and then pausing long enough to toss her unceremoniously over his shoulder. Then he was off again, running hard, each jolt punching air out of her lungs. When she looked up, through the trees, she saw Salazar's *Los Piratas*. God, she didn't want to be caught again.

For a big man, he was agile, leaping over broken logs, barreling through brush. He waded into water, strode across like he was on ice. When he hit shore, he made the incline of the bank without effort. Suddenly he whisked her off his shoulder, and when her feet hit the ground, he steadied her with a steely arm around her waist. He pushed her against the trunk of a tree, and her back slammed against the bark. He pressed his body against hers, completely immobilizing her. Completely shielding her, protecting her from the men after them. Her heart lurched.

Adrenaline washed into her veins on a river of stark, icy fear.

She went to speak, but a powerful hand clamped over her mouth. "Don't say a word." His voice was soft and gravelly, and very close to her ear, his breath blowing across her skin as he spoke. "We're going up."

She managed a sharp nod.

"Good. Now take a breath. I'll boost you. Don't move once you get in the branches." He spoke so quietly, she had to strain to hear him. She had to focus on him, focus on his breathing and slow down her own.

It wasn't going to happen. Not as long as her heart was

racing, totally at odds with the steady beat of his. She felt him against her chest. He wasn't crushing or hurting her. It was very effective, what he was doing, and made her diligently attended self-defense classes moot. He had immobilized her in one second flat. She felt engulfed between him and the tree.

His body was warm, very hard against hers, and if she wasn't mistaken, the cool, steely ridge she felt against her hip was a handgun. A quip about him being glad to see her made her smile even in the face of fear. This was no time for flirting.

The imprint of it had slowly registered over the last few seconds, and now she was sure this man was doubly armed and dangerous.

He turned her, manhandled her body as he boosted her up to the lowest branch. She grabbed onto the thick, leafy lifeline and thanked all those free weights at the gym for the arm strength to pull herself up the rest of the way, his hands giving her a base to push from. Climbing higher to give him room, she watched in awe as he simply nudged his gun to his back and crouched. With an explosive jump, gear, pack, and all two hundred pounds of man latched onto the branch, and seemingly without effort, he chin-upped his way onto the branch.

He settled next to her and with his thumb, motioned for her to climb higher. She did, and he followed until they were nestled in the crotch of a huge branch.

He pulled her close to him, and she didn't protest. He was all that stood between her and those men out there. She had no idea if they wanted her back, but Salazar had been adamant that she was to be treated carefully and kept alive. She was his conduit to the media.

But they would kill Ruckus. There was no doubt in her mind.

He was close, and she was so scared it took a couple of seconds for his face to register. When it did, she couldn't quite catch her breath, and it had nothing to do with the men down below looking for them. Deep-set, blue I-mean-business eyes beneath sable lashes and the straight dark line of his eyebrows all formed drop-dead gorgeous features. He had to be in his mid-thirties, the lines of his face more defined around the eyes and mouth. His gaze was down toward the ground, but she kept hers on him. His shoulders were very broad, tapering down to a slim waist, so many things on the vest he wore across his wide chest.

His gaze rose to meet her clearly assessing one. The slight lift of his eyebrows seemed confrontational until the slow slide of his gaze over her face and the brief moment it spent focused on her mouth made her reassess that look. A shiver went down her spine at the clear and present danger this man presented.

He was trouble in the man department, that was for sure. The kind of guy who took and demanded. An alpha. She'd come into contact with plenty of them when she'd been a war correspondent. The military was full of them. And special operators, they were eat-you-for-lunch alpha.

Then he looked down, and the intense expression on his face had her dropping her eyes. Between the wide branches of the tree, she saw enough to make her heart slam back up into overdrive.

Men were walking slowly through the brush, moving silently through the shadows. His hand went over her mouth a split second before she involuntarily gasped. He was totally focused on the men. A bead of sweat trickled down the side of her face, and her knees started to tremble.

The air was filled once again with something terrible, a portent of violence that she didn't want any part of. If they looked up, could they make them out in the dark?

Every muscle in Ruckus's body was taut, ready. He leveled his weapon and aimed it down. Dana got a sick feeling in her stomach.

There was ferocity in every line of his body, and the strength of him, the readiness of him turned her on.

The idea slid through her like a jolt of electricity. She was not going to get involved with him—if the opportunity even presented itself. Where had that crazy thought come from? She didn't know a thing about him, except he was the complete opposite of everything she had ever known. A warrior. The real thing, a soldier who put his life on the line for people he didn't know, served his country and kept her and what she so dearly loved safe.

And there was Jeffrey. Of course, there was Jeffrey. She'd been with him for a year. Okay, so most of that year she'd been traveling. Ruckus finally released her mouth but put his finger to his lips. Salazar's men had passed underneath them and were now moving off into the distance.

But he wouldn't let her move or talk, and she was just fine with that. Finally, he said in a low tone, "They've moved off. Where are you guys?"

He listened intently. "Are the choppers there?" Nodding, he said, "I'll be fine. I'll get the information I need and check in. Get out of here for now. I'll be in touch."

Then he looked at her. "Time to move, honey."

"I'm not your honey," she whispered as she disengaged her legs and gave him a caustic look. There was no way he was going to ditch her, and if he did, she knew exactly where Salazar had gone. She was going to get her memory cards back come hell, high water, or Ruckus.

She gingerly made her way to the lowest branch of the tree. "Wait here," he ordered, then grabbed the branch and swung down to the ground with surprisingly little sound.

He gestured up to her. "Jump down. I'll catch you."

"I can make it."

"And twist an ankle in the process. No. Jump."

"Did anyone ever tell you you're a bossy jerk?"

He stared up at her as if he could burn holes into wood with that laser glare. "They can't. They have to follow my orders."

"Right. You're GI Joes."

"We're SEALs, Dana. Not army."

"Oh, I'm so sorry I insulted you when you've done nothing but distrust me and drag me through the jungle, pushing and shoving."

"Would you rather I'd left you to your *friends*?"

"No, but that's not the point."

He opened his arms and his mouth hardened. "Jump, cupcake. I don't have all day."

"Cupcake," she grumbled and did as he instructed, landing firmly in his big grasp. He held her for a moment. Jeez the man was built, the muscles of his arms and chest hard against her. She could feel every breath he took. He was invading her personal space. Not by holding her—that was necessary—but with those eyes of his, gunmetal blue, and this close she could see a navy blue rim around the iris. Those eyes... Now that she could see how thickly lashed they were, they made her breath suddenly feel trapped in her chest. Being this close to him made it hard to think with any clarity.

She cursed the camo paint on his face, wanting to see his features clearly, the dark also hampering her vision. But his

lips were finely defined in the stubble on his face, accentu-
ating the fullness.

"I'm not a cupcake," she said firmly, but it came out
much too breathless. "I am a reporter and a former war
correspondent." She had calmly reported the news as the
chaos of battle exploded around her. She'd dealt with military men on a daily basis, SEALs included. So what was it
about this man, this Ruckus, that made her lose her cool?

A twinkle entered his eyes that was either a trick in the
dark or was utterly wicked. "Soft, slightly moist and very
sweet...cupcake."

Okay, that was wicked, purely wicked, wicked man.

"Light as one, too," he murmured.

"Sugar is bad for your health. So, put me down, Rambo."

"It's Ruckus," he said, his expression telling her he knew
she'd given him the wrong nickname on purpose, a way to
subtly dig at him and get some distance. He shifted her,
making her far too aware of his hands. When he released
her legs and shifted his arm to the small of her back as he
lowered her slowly to the ground, her awareness when her
thighs brushed along his filled her senses, and she clutched
at his shoulders for balance. But he was rock solid and had
no intention of letting her fall. Before she could step back,
he now deliberately filled up her personal space, reaching
out. Not sure of his intentions, she went still rather than
move away, her breath trapped in her chest again, but he
only removed leaves out of her hair.

"Oh, my mistake." She felt like an idiot. They didn't have
time for this crap in the middle of all this danger.

"I think we're safe now. We should get going. SERE
time." Damn his voice was deep, smooth. Her gaze dipped to
his mouth, unbidden, and she had to fight the urge to wet
her lips.

"Dana?"

The way he said her name with that gruff quality made her senses flare again. This was going to be a pain in her ass. "Uh...yes. We—we should get going." She stuttered her reply and was glad it was so dark. "What is SERE?"

"Survival, Evasion, Resistance, Escape, but we're more interested in evasion. We need to go north."

"Right. That's where Yaviza is." She looked up briefly and then said, "It's this way." She stepped in the right direction, and his hand landed on her arm.

"Let me lead in case we run into some stragglers." He moved in front of her, that broad back effectively obscuring her vision. Geez, he was big, and she wanted to kick him, get rid of this...this...attraction. "How did you know which way was north without a compass?"

She huffed a laugh. "The north star. I know how to navigate. I'm pretty self-sufficient when men aren't kidnapping me or chasing me with guns and dragging me through the jungle."

He grunted and that was the extent of his answer. After about an hour and a half, he abruptly stopped. Judging by the position of the moon, she figured it was about three in the morning.

"We're not going to get there by running ourselves ragged," he said. "We'll camp for the rest of the night and get a fresh start in the morning. "What provisions do you have in your pack?"

"I have a tent, blanket, cooking utensils, a way to start a fire, but I know that's out of the question. Besides, I don't have any food with me. I also have a change of clothes, first aid kit, rain poncho, camera, bug spray, personal hygiene stuff and makeup."

He chuckled at the last one. "Pull out the tent, and you're

right, we can't make a fire. I could probably hunt us up something, but we don't want to broadcast our position to anyone looking for us. A fire can be seen from quite a distance. Looks like it's MREs for us."

She released her pack and swung it around. "Oh, Meals, Ready-to-Eat." She'd heard plenty about them but hadn't ever had one. Before she could open her pack and pull out the tent, he took it out of her hands and searched in a side pocket where she'd put the IDs, passports and press credentials.

Pulling them out, he flashed a small light over the documents. He looked up at her face, then back down. "Looks like you and your crew are who you say you are."

She snatched her papers back. "I am, and you could have asked me. Do you want to frisk me for weapons?"

"Nope. I watched you get dressed, cupcake. I've seen all your weapons."

"Don't call me cupcake, you jerk. Don't you have any decency?"

"Sure." He shrugged. "But when it comes to combat and the red zone, I go commando. That's the nature of this job."

"And demeaning women with cutesy names is your way of keeping me firmly in the detached package sort of way you SEALs think?"

He scowled, which seemed to be his permanent facial expression. "Women are easily as combative as men and are sneakier about it. I don't trust anyone. But if it comes down to it, Dana, no one is going to harm you unless I ain't breathing. And if that happens, I got a feeling you're one tough cupcake and won't go down without a fight. I think I could pass for Nelson if I need to. It was lucky all of them were packaged together."

She nodded.

He went to pull out the tent, and she slapped his hands away, his comments making her even more breathless and so aware of him, not only as a man, but as a warrior and a good judge of character. He gave her a narrowed-eye look, then sighed when she glared back and raised her chin. She assembled it her-own-damn-self, and when she was finished, she turned to find him pulling out foil packets.

Holding them up, he said, "Spaghetti and meatballs. You're in a for a treat." But the sarcastic lilt to his voice warned her that whatever was contained in those packets was anything but a treat.

3

She was a definite hoo-yah on the sexy scale. It's not what he should have been thinking right now. In fact, he should be grilling her on Salazar's whereabouts. That ex-patriot turned drug lord wasn't going to escape the noose that was tightening around his neck.

This woman couldn't have landed into a darker den. Salazar was American, rich, and a deadly drug thug with international ties and body counts on his resume. War correspondent or not, this little sweet treat was out of her league.

He realized that she wasn't a lightweight. She'd kept up and performed with an amazing quickness. He'd called her cupcake to get her back up and make it that much easier to carry out his plan. She hadn't disappointed him. Dana Sorenson, aka cupcake, put him in his place, but she was right about one thing. He didn't trust women. Period.

It could have been because all the women in his life had betrayed him. He couldn't extend his trust that far anymore. The only place he was safe was in his band of brothers. The SEAL team was his family.

So, he was interested in her body. Who wouldn't be? He was a red-blooded American male, and his appetites were a little raunchier than the average guy. Dana had some dangerous weapons just as he said, and he wouldn't hesitate to fuck her. Why the hell not? She was hot. He gritted his teeth. *Yeah, Cooper. It's easier to objectify her than interact with her one on one. Much easier to think about her as nothing but a female body.*

She eyed the packet he held up with a dubious eye, and he didn't blame her, although the spaghetti choice was a good one. It tasted like the canned variety but packed with many more calories. Also included in the meal was au gratin potatoes, carrot pound cake, crackers, cheese spread and a grape electrolyte beverage.

He got to preparing them with the heating pack they came with. The instructions were hilarious, especially the warning that the heating pack was inedible.

"You can heat up the entrees?"

"Yeah, believe me, it's better that way."

She sat down cross-legged as he tucked the foil packet into the heat pouch and folded it over. The chemical reaction was fast, and the heater stayed hot for about ten minutes, letting him move on to the potatoes when the spaghetti pack was done.

He had every intention of getting the information he needed out of her and dropping her shapely ass at the airport to make sure she got safely on a plane to the States before he went after Salazar.

"My crew—"

"Are safely out."

"Where did they take them?"

"Classified information but know they will get medical attention and escort back to the US."

"They both knew the risks, but I'm worried about James. I sure hope he'll be okay."

"He will, or he won't." After serving for the number of years he had, that was reality. People died every day, sometimes in his arms. It was the nature of this job. "No use worrying about it."

"Are you really that detached?"

He stiffened. "No, I'm a realist." He shoved her portion into her hands and said, "Eat. Then get some sleep. We're heading out at the crack of dawn." He didn't want to analyze too closely all the emotions he'd wrapped up from all the death he'd seen. It would overwhelm him, and as a SEAL, he was always in control of everything.

He started eating his.

It took her a few more minutes as she scrutinized him. He wished she wouldn't speculate about him at all. She didn't know him. He'd compartmentalized everything from his childhood to his marriage to his last deployment. Women were soft creatures, a lot of work, duplicitous, and manipulating. But damn if she wasn't freaking beautiful, those eyes of hers boring into his.

As a news person, she was probably pretty good at reading people. Not this SEAL. He'd keep his secrets.

Her first bite was tentative. She tasted it delicately, and he couldn't help watching her lips as her jaw moved. She looked at him. "It's not bad."

"Yeah, one of my favorites along with beef stew and some of the snacks. You'll need the calories. It's only one thousand since we had to share."

She sat up straight. "Two thousand? In one small meal?"

"Yup. More than you consume in one day, I'm sure."

"I don't count calories. I eat whatever I want, especially cookies. Chocolate chip is my favorite. It's all about moderation. Besides, I'm a runner. Normally, I can run for miles without breaking a sweat. I really didn't need carrying. I just—"

"Panicked."

She huffed out a breath. "Yes, I panicked."

He was surprised. He expected her to lie. Most people did about fear. Fear made someone vulnerable, and most people didn't like that—especially him. "Bullets flying tends to do that." He wondered if she was as honest about this. What exactly would she lie about? Everyone had secrets. Some were so buried they weren't accessible, but they were there beneath the surface, screwing up the head. "Where exactly did Salazar go?"

"I'd rather not say. I don't want to wake up and have you gone. I said I was going with you, and I meant it."

Ruckus leaned forward, his tone soft and deadly. "For the record, cupcake, I wouldn't leave a civilian stranded in the deep jungle with no food or water, hostiles everywhere. No matter how capable or a pain in the ass she was being."

She smiled sweetly. "My hero."

He stiffened, her words reminding him completely of his past and how not a hero he was. "Are you always this much trouble?"

She didn't bat a lash. He found himself utterly fascinated with her face and every emotion that crossed it. It pissed him off. He wondered how she would look when she was being done good. She wasn't about to let him close enough to touch her, let alone do her. "Only with you, it seems."

He gave her his best I'm-the-one-in-charge look that scared the crap out of just about anyone. Still nothing. "It's not personal. You are interfering with a federal package here. There could be repercussions from the attorney general on down."

Her eyes widened and she cooed. "Not the attorney general. What are they going to do? Dig up my tax returns? I have the first amendment on my side. I'm a journalist, and this is free speech. So stuff that in your kit bag."

"I wouldn't put it past them," he muttered. "There are many ways to retaliate. Least of all screwing up your passport. They could throw you in jail for a long time." He certainly didn't want to imagine this beauty behind bars because she was being difficult. What was driving her to go after those memory cards besides the story? Was she that one-minded? But getting personal was out of the question. He didn't want to get into her head or have her get into his.

"Salazar has my property, and I'm getting it back." She bulldozed ahead without taking a breath, and he half expected her to poke his chest. "I'm not asking your permission. I'm just stating facts." She did poke him, but in his tactical vest right in the center of his chest. No disappointment there. "For me. This is *personal*."

"Are you sure this has nothing to do with getting all this recorded for a story?"

She froze and turned around. "A story! You act like this is nightly news. I don't do stories. I do real life and the suffering and pain that goes with that. Those people deserve to have that in the limelight, so others are aware of what is really going on. My interviews, their heartache, pain, suffering and hope for freedom are on those cards. They're irreplaceable! I don't care whether you think that's important or not."

He grabbed her arm, ready to give her a dose of reality. "The average person doesn't give a damn what's going on." Okay, so she was a do-gooder, and he'd made a mistake when he pegged her for a news hound.

She pulled out of his grasp, stumbling. When he went to

help steady her, she moved shakily away. "I do, and I'm reporting it. At least I will reach some people. That's enough for me." She walked a few steps away, then whirled around. "I'm taking you to Salazar, so technically, I am cooperating. You're just pissed you're not in control. But you can arrest me at the crack of dawn, Rambo. I'm going to sleep."

He gritted his teeth and wanted to yell at the top of his lungs, but it would be too dangerous as he watched her shapely backside disappear into the tent. He angrily snatched up the remnants of their meal and buried everything. Then he grabbed his M4 and sat down, bracing his back against a tree staring out into the night. She was determined to risk her life for those cards. Dammit! "Freaking irritating cupcake," he muttered.

"You got yourself a situation, LT?" Kid's amused voice buzzed in his ear.

Ruckus sat up, his body tense. "Where are you, petty officer?"

"At the LZ. All the bad guys are gone or dead. We're not leaving here without you. I thought I made that clear."

"You wet behind the ears little bastard," he snarled. "I told you to get back to the carrier with those civilians. I would get in touch."

"Copy that, sir," Scarecrow's smooth Southern voice came over the comm. "You absolutely didn't say anything about us coming back. We went to the carrier and dropped off the friendlies just like you ordered. The doc said the unconscious guy, James Quinn, has a severe concussion and is dehydrated. He's getting fluids and they're assessing his condition. Liam Nelson is also dehydrated and malnourished. Cuts, bruises, and a broken wrist, but he'll mend. Now we're here for backup. Just let us know what's shaking, and we'll do what's needed."

"Also, Major McRae wants you to get the information out of the reporter and then get her to safety, pronto."

"Good luck with that, LT," Blue said, and the rest of them chuckled.

He pinched the bridge of his nose. Apparently, he was being usurped on every front. "You chuckleheads having a good time? Good. Stand by then. I will let you know the moment I have Salazar's coordinates."

"The little...ah...cupcake sandbagging you, Ruckus?" Cowboy twanged. In the open mic, he heard chuckles. Damn them. This wasn't funny.

He looked toward the tent. "Nothing I can't handle." The little *cupcake* was a handful and seemingly not at all intimidated by him or the US government. He didn't want to, but he had to wonder what was driving her. Was this really about some migrant story? Or was there more here he just didn't know about? Didn't want to know about. He had a directive. Get Salazar alive, but Dana would take precedence over that slime dog. There were no detours, no barricades, nothing he wouldn't do to carry out his mission. One beautiful woman with a steel attitude certainly wasn't going to stop him. He chewed metal for dessert.

He took several battle naps during the rest of the night, alert for any sound that would indicate tangos. In the early morning, the air hung thickly, though cooler, almost dense to the touch. He listened carefully as he surveyed the area, picking out the movement of little creatures separate from his own breathing. They watched him intently, well aware of a predator when they saw one. He had to give them their due. Surviving in this jungle when even the plants could kill was not a small feat.

He went to the nearest water source and filled his camelback, a soft skinned water container with a straw that allowed him to drink on the move, keeping his hands free. He purified it with tablets. Then using the soap he found in Dana's pack, he washed the camo paint off his face, the breeze blowing across his wet hair and skin, cooling him.

He climbed the nearest tree with his palm-sized binoculars, a Cyclops version. He tested the movement of the auto-focus, then scanned the area once, starting closest to them, systematically clearing the area of threat before moving away. Ruckus swung to the right, lower in the valley. Movement was sporadic, the flutter of birds darting everywhere, their feathers flashes of bright color in the gloom, flitting among the lacework of the branches. Monkeys contrasted their fluttering with powerful holds of disproportionately long limbs and prehensile tails, tree branches bending beneath their weight, their black and brown hides all but lost in the foliage, only glimpses of their white faces visible.

Some of them watched Ruckus from a nearby tree, their faces intent. The humans had miles and miles of this jungle to cover, filled to the brim with danger. Too bad they couldn't use the trees the same way, Tarzan style. The safest place for her would be Yaviza, far to the north. He'd have to get the information he needed by the time he got there. Then she could be on her way back to the US, and he'd be closer to his original target.

Charm wasn't his strong suit. He was more of a blunt force trauma kind of guy.

She came out of the tent and looked around. For a moment, her face showed her surprise, and then panic. She really thought he'd abandoned her. He couldn't let her think that. Even after her opposing behavior, he knew exactly what abandonment felt like. He whistled softly, and she jerked her face toward the tree he was sitting in. Relief replaced that look, and for all her bravado, she was scared.

With a wash of protectiveness flowing over him, he stared down at her. She shielded her eyes and stared back. For better or worse, she was his charge, and he had no intention of letting her get hurt, no matter how much she was holding back from him.

After one last look, he started to climb down, then movement far away caught his attention. A drug caravan, boats moving through the jungle at a slow pace. He wouldn't say no to some transportation but messing with those drug smugglers whether they were CLP or another organization could very well reveal their location to Salazar's men who were no doubt scouring the jungle for them.

It was clear that Dana was important to their leader, and Salazar wasn't known for his forgiveness or mercy. They wouldn't give up. Their lives were on the line. Well, all of them would have to freaking go through him. No one was harming a hair on that beauty's head.

He climbed down. They would eat some more of the MREs and then get going. They had many miles to cover.

As HIS BOOTS hit the ground, she approached him. His back was to her. He pushed away from the trunk and turned to face her.

"Good…" The word *morning* didn't emerge because her throat muscles contracted and all the oxygen she needed to speak simply backed up in her lungs. Ruckus's coffee-brown hair gleamed in the sun, auburn highlights flaming in the dark strands. With his helmet off and that camo paint washed clean from his features, she discovered that this SEAL was as drop-dead gorgeous as his face hinted in the darkness.

The bright light of day lovingly revealed that his eyes were indeed a gunmetal blue, a dark rim outlining the iris and emphasizing his steely gaze. The expression on his lean, tanned face was stern, almost brooding.

He leaned against the tree, but the energy in him just wouldn't let him relax enough for the trunk to take his full weight.

He dropped his head back, looking at her from beneath his thick tangle of lashes. "You thought I left you," he said softly instead of in that gruff, I'm-deadly voice he'd used last night to argue with her. Then he unfurled a grin that knocked her back as if she'd been punched in the stomach, as if he'd reached out and touched her skin, trailing his fingertips in an intimate way that had her heart beating double time.

Never had she ever felt this blindsided by a set of dimples and a high wattage smile. He really should do that more often...all the time. It transformed his face. Even though it registered in his eyes, it couldn't quite do away with the dark intensity there.

"For a moment, I did. Then I realized you wouldn't do that."

"No, I told you I wouldn't." He gestured in the distance. "If you have to go, do it over there. We'll want everything... localized so we can remove every trace we were here."

"Go?"

"To the lady's room," he said delicately.

She set her hands on her hips, caught off guard. "Oh, I see. You even decide where I do my business?"

The smile faded from his face and his brows dropped. "What? It's for our—"

"Gotcha," she intoned and backed up as his face cleared,

then he dropped his head and chuckled. Okay, so he could take a joke.

She took care of going, and when she came back, he was preparing more of the MREs. His face was in profile and she got punched all over again. He was back to looking stern and tough. Annoyed with herself for even noticing his looks, she gritted her teeth. He was kneeling, his big hands on his thighs, that automatic weapon easily within his reach. She knelt down too, starving.

"What treat do you have for me this morning?"

"Eggs, bacon and toast with a side of fruit."

She huffed a whimsical breath. "What are you? A miracle worker?"

"No, sorry. It's just more MREs. But I do have fruit. Zapplesauce." He held up the container.

"Zapplesauce," she said, her voice tentative.

"An amped up applesauce, supplement charged, complex carbohydrate that will give us a turbo charge. If you're really good and we can find a safe place to heat water, we'll get a chance at Irish-cream coffee later."

She snorted. "Oookkkaaayyy."

He laughed and started the heating process for the pork sausage patty and chocolate toaster pastry. He opened the package for wheat snack bread and blackberry jam, and the orange electrolyte beverage, giving her half of everything.

"Thank you for sharing your food with me."

They were nearly at eye level, and Dana felt herself leaning toward him, as if he were drawing her by some powerful magnetic force. His gaze slid down to her mouth and lingered there, frank in its appraisal. She swallowed hard and barely managed to resist running her tongue across her bottom lip.

He looked away and blew out a breath. She had to take

one of her own. As he ripped open packages and prepared the meal, his mouth was set in stern lines again above a strong, stubborn-looking chin that sported an inch-long diagonal scar. He looked tough and dangerous suddenly, and she wanted him to smile again. His gaze came back to hers as he handed her the heated meal; the touch of his hand, warm and rough, sent a shiver down her spine.

"How long have you been in the SEALs?" she asked to get her mind off his arresting face, off her speculation of what he looked like beneath that uniform.

His gaze held hers fast. He looked every inch the warrior and not much inclined to give her a whole lot of personal information.

"Twenty years."

She waited for him to elaborate, but he didn't, just started eating. That couldn't be right.

"That long? You don't look old enough to be forty."

"I'm not. I'm thirty-seven."

"Oh, that means you went in when you were...seventeen. Wow, that's young."

"You're very good at math," he responded, continuing to eat.

"Why?"

He glanced at her and then down to his meal. "You almost done? We need to get going."

"I thought a little conversation would help. Getting to know each other—"

"Is a waste of time and energy. We're only going to be together until I get you home. So stop trying to interview me."

Anger flared at his tone. "I'm not interviewing you. I was just asking questions like a normal human being," she huffed out and then stood up. He stood up so quickly, she had to back up a step. He shifted his weight forward, suddenly invading her personal space, and she had to fight to keep from jumping back as her tension level rose to the red zone. She gulped down her instinctive reaction at his defensiveness. In her experience, it covered pain and unhappiness. Tilting her chin to look at him, she stood her ground. She'd faced down men like him without batting an eyelash, handled mortars and IED blasts, dealt with living in a war zone for years. She wanted to know at least one personal thing about him. She couldn't figure out why. Maybe it made this more of a partnership than him barking orders and deciding the course of action. "I don't even know your name," she murmured.

"You don't need to know my name, cupcake. I'm clandestine and under the radar here. The less you know, the better. Classified is classified for a reason."

"I already know your mission."

"Yeah, because you were caught in the middle between Salazar and a bunch of Navy SEALs. We're not out here on a pleasure walk. I'm going to get him. That's all you need to know."

He started gathering everything up and left to where he'd designated their latrine. After a few moments, he came back. She'd already broken down the tent and stowed it back in her pack. He stoically grabbed his pack and swung it onto his back. She figured it must weigh sixty pounds. "I can tell you your team is in stable condition and the prognosis is optimistic."

She nodded, grateful for the information. Grabbing up his weapon, he started off.

She followed his retreating back.

～

RUCKUS CLENCHED HIS JAW. First off because he was such an asshole to her, but secondly because she made him feel vulnerable, made him think about why he'd gone into the navy at seventeen. Stuff he didn't want to remember. Normally, he was careful and gentle with the opposite sex, but Dana was pushing buttons he didn't even know he had. Most women backed off when he closed down, but not her. She had to keep asking her personal questions. He just wasn't going to get involved with her on that level. He was her escort through to safety, and she had knowledge he needed. That was all.

He would focus on the fastest route to his target. They needed one of those boats.

"We're going to head toward the FARC and procure one of their boats. I figure we should get there by nightfall after stopping for food and water."

"You're going to steal a boat from the FARC? That's not exactly done."

He turned to her. "If you can't solve a problem, it's because you're playing by the rules," he murmured. SEALs thought outside the box and did what needed to be done, rules of engagement be damned.

"I had safe passage with the FARC." She gave a self-deprecating laugh. "Well, safe is probably a misnomer, but, nevertheless, they allowed us through. It was required to go into the Gap and get my story."

"Consorting with drug runners and murderers? That's very un-cupcake-like of you."

She glared at him, not at all amused. "There's always two sides of the argument, but it was a necessary evil. They would say they were patriots fighting for their country," she said through gritted teeth. "It kills me we had to ask permission of them to get what was necessary. They have been drug-running their cocaine for years to avoid the sea patrols, creating trouble for the indigenous people here. They force them to act as guides, too."

"It's perfect for FARC. It's treacherous, swampy, and nobody really lives out here."

"Yes, I guess it is. I could talk to them. I still have their permission to move freely through here."

He turned to her. "But I don't. I'm a Navy SEAL on foreign soil on a black op. I can't let anyone know I'm here. We're on our own," he said, and her face blanched.

He wanted to feed her a nice, safe story, but the fact remained that every moment they traversed this jungle, they were vulnerable. She had backbone and courage. He would give her that, but in the end, it wouldn't matter. Maybe he didn't want to get personal, but he admired her. She would go back to her life and he'd get on with the business of protecting America. He'd never see her again.

He ignored the regret at that thought and led her into the undergrowth.

4

The black water gleamed like glass under the light of a partial moon. Huge trees, thick on each bank, straight and dark, loomed above the jungle floor. In the near distance, thunder rolled and lightning flashed pink behind a bank of clouds. South, Dana thought automatically, her feet carefully placed, picking her way up the slippery bank. A storm was coming up from South America.

God, she was tired after having walked all day, her nerves raw from the constant vigilance. How he kept his focus so tight for the twelve hours they'd been moving impressed the hell out of her.

As she continued to move ahead, Ruckus nothing but a big, dusky shadow ahead of her, the sheer wall of jungle surrounding them, hampering their movements, seemed alive, a world unto itself, ancient, mysterious, primal. It seemed more of an entity than an ecosystem. The violence seeped into the ground, the sound of agonized cries absorbed into the leaves, bark, moss and very air around them. Something dark and twisted born from the hostility and the violence here, something with a mind and eyes and a dark, shadowed soul. That impression closed in on her, and she took deep breaths, thinking about her mother's hushed voice singing a lullaby. Even as she lay dying in that hospital bed, it was her mom who had comforted her.

Squeezing her eyes closed, she breathed around her need to get those memory cards back. Her work had been consecrated with her mother's suffering. Dana had missed seeing her one last time because she'd been half a world away reporting on the suffering of others. Those memory cards held the stories, but they weren't just stories. They documented real people, real pain, real suffering, and... Dana's throat tightened...real courage. It was a homage to her mom and Dana's terrible missed opportunity to say goodbye.

She was sure somewhere in the dark, somewhere close by, bodies lay, the violence not seen but felt, seeping into her like the cold, and she shivered and rubbed her hands over her arms as an image flashed through her head. Bodies lying out here, alone, dead, the jungle watching, knowing, keeping its secrets...

"Why the hell are you lagging?"

Ruckus's voice snapped the terrible vision, and she jumped. When she didn't immediately answer, he covered the short space between them. She shivered.

"Dana?" He studied her. "Are you cold?"

She nodded once.

"It's a mind-set, babe."

"It's a biological function, *Rambo*," she countered angrily because sparring with him kept her aware and staying aware was keeping her alive.

"Fuck science. We keep moving. Get your head around that. Keep your goal in mind. Hector Salazar. He's the bastard."

She shivered, unable to stop the involuntary action.

"Damn," he swore as the first drops of rain fell. Grumbling about women, jungles, rain and inconveniences, he pulled his pack from his back, and with quick, efficient, irritated moves, he opened it and dug around inside. Finally he retrieved a waterproof poncho. Without saying anything, he rose and pulled it none to gently over her head. As the rain started to fall faster, he stared at her for a moment, the warm lights of concern in his eyes giving away what he was thinking. He cared about what happened to her, that was no surprise. He was a SEAL; they protected people, and it was part of their job. But it was his personal concern for her, not some nondescript HVT or noncombatant. Her heart jumped, then thundered in her chest. She hadn't even liked him from the start, but how could she want him so damn bad if she didn't at least feel something for him? Then he grabbed her arm, his grip firm but gentle. "Let's move. We don't have any time to play in the water puddles," he growled.

They heard voices and Ruckus dragged her behind a huge tree. "I'll be right back." He disappeared, *poof*, like a magician, and when he came back, he scared the living hell right out of her. She hadn't heard a thing.

"Soon we'll be motoring the rest of the way to Yaviza."

"You still plan to steal one?"

"Yeah, there's plenty of them hanging around, and I'd prefer not to waste ammo."

"Waste ammo..." Her breath backed up into her lungs. Then she heard a familiar voice and an idea formed. "What if I talked to them alone? Asked them for a boat. Then you wouldn't have to steal it, and we wouldn't have them pissed at us, too." They were currently standing a safe distance away from a group of FARC. They had several boats on the shore of the river. Dana couldn't tell if anything was in the boats, but she was certain that she could talk to the dark man dressed in a green shirt with a semi-automatic slung to his back.

"What if they decide you're worth more than a boat?"

"Why would they do that? I have documentation that I'm free to move around the Gap. It comes from their leaders in Cuba. I recognize one of them. He helped us when we first arrived. I'm sure he'll remember me."

"I'm sure any guy with eyes would remember you," he muttered. Dana wasn't sure if that was a compliment or not. Then, he shook his head. "Do you think because he recognizes you, that's going to stop them from taking you hostage and demanding a ransom from your family? Everything in this place is about money. You've seen it on your journey with those migrants. They don't give a damn about human life. Everyone is expendable to keep those cocaine profits flowing. People here are robbed blind, made to be mules and stripped of everything they have. If they're not murdered, they're left destitute."

That brought her up short. He was aware of what was going on here? She looked up at him, and the dark canopy smothered all the ambient light so that his handsome face was nothing but a dark silhouette in the night. But she knew those features. Her fingers ached to trace that mouth and just simply stare into those blue eyes that sucked at her soul. They had differences, and he was bossy and pushy, grumpy and testy. But she saw something. It was like staring into the face of death. There was no looking away. She knew there was something lurking in his past that drove him as much as her past drove her. He wasn't a one-sided, unemotional jerk at all. And that made her stomach jolt.

Not such an egocentric man as she first thought. Her

estimation of him went up a notch. Which, in light of her physical attraction to him, wasn't helping. "I'm not trusting blindly here. They have already helped me and my crew."

He started to crowd her, and before she knew it, her back came up against the rough trunk of a tree. The solid barrier behind her and a hard, muscled, intense man in front of her. He pressed his hand to the bark and leaned forward, getting all up into her personal space. Most likely a male tactic to intimidate. But Dana didn't feel intimidated. She felt hot and bothered, achy and needy, his close proximity not having the desired effect at all.

"Listen, I understand where you're coming from. One boat out of many won't be that big a deal. But if they decide to extract money out of you or your family, then I'm dealing with you in the middle of a large number of armed men. Because, cupcake, I'm not leaving you behind. You're coming with me, frosting and all. It's a freaking risk."

"A freaking calculated risk. We already have the CLP after us. We don't need the FARC, too. You're trained to deal with armed men, and I've been in plenty of situations I've managed to talk myself out of. Look around. There are at least twenty of them. The boats are guarded, and the river is teeming with alligators."

"You think it's the armed men I'm worried about." His voice sent shivers down her spine. "When the bullets start flying, the only bodies that will be hitting the ground will be theirs."

Her eyes drifted closed and she took a soft breath. Somehow, that was not a very comforting thought that one man could deliver so much violence, especially when he uttered his comment in such a stone-cold tone of voice. She got it. SEALs were take-charge guys and most likely didn't like to be second guessed. Standing there, boxed in with his big body, the view blocked by those shoulders and that chest drove it home to her that he was large and wanted to be in charge.

He was definitely built. Dirty and sweaty, scruffy stubble along his jaw, but as of right now he was The Great Wall of China, and she wasn't going through him or around him. Not even a horde of Huns could breach those fortifications.

"We'll wait until nightfall and—"

She took another breath. "Look, Rambo. I—"

"It's Ruckus," he said through gritted teeth.

"I might call you something else if I knew your real name," she hissed, her voice low. He shook his head. "You know mine," she insisted.

"I wish I didn't."

That stung a bit, and he'd said it like he'd rather be anywhere than here with her. And, if she had her preference, she would be anywhere other than here, too. He was six feet, two inches of an immovable object, and unless she talked Mr. You Don't Need to Know My Real Name into letting her have a go at getting a boat, it wasn't happening. For better or worse, they were partners in this odyssey to find Salazar. Her determination was as deep and immovable as his.

The FARC were organized, had an uneasy relationship with the clan, but it was still peaceful between them. It would only get ugly if territory was going to be in dispute. The area in question would be the drug routes. Dana was aware that Salazar was going to expand, and he was going to do it either by negotiation or by blood. He'd made that clear in his interview.

She was just about to agree to do it his way when someone called out in Spanish. "Who's there? Show yourself!"

Ruckus backed up and grabbed his weapon. She pantomimed with her thumb, and his mouth tightened but he gave her a curt nod. Dana called out, "Captain Escobar? Is that you?"

He gave her a fierce look, his eyes shooting daggers, and backed up. She mouthed she was sorry and his eyes narrowed. There was no way they could run, and if keeping Ruckus a secret was imperative, then she would have to brazen this out. It wasn't optimal, but she was sure she could get the boat, pull over to shore, and get him aboard. Then they could be on their way to Yaviza.

She had no illusions it would be smooth sailing all the way. She'd have more battles with this man before they parted company. He hadn't budged but was still concealed from the man with the mean looking rifle pointed directly at her. He literally melted into nothing, and she took a hard breath.

She came out from behind the tree, her hands up. She knew the drill. The shadows were deepening across the jungle, melding into one darkness, the veil of night spreading from the horizon. Certain the air was blue behind her from the quiet swearing her navy SEAL was doing in his head, she took a step toward the man who held a rifle to his shoulder.

"Escobar!" the man shouted, the sound of it carrying to the water and the boats. His dark, intense eyes never left her. She didn't recognize him, and he wasn't dressed like the FARC. An uneasiness crawled across her skin.

The swarthy Cuban materialized through the trees, and his face split into a wide, white grin. "Ms. Sorenson. What happened? Did you get lost? We put you in a boat, and it was a straight ride up the river."

"No, but I'm in a bind."

The man who was covering her didn't immediately lower his weapon, but Captain Escobar touched the barrel of the gun, and the rebel dropped it to his side.

"Let us talk someplace more comfortable." Holding out his hand, she took it and he drew her out of the jungle into a small clearing. She had no idea where Ruckus was, but she was confident he was close, watching. That made her feel safer.

There were a few tents and remnants of a meal. He led her to a small backless folding chair not far from the boats. She glanced at them in the deepening gloom, but still couldn't see inside any of them.

"Have you eaten?"

"No."

He waved his hand, and someone dished up a plate of stew. It smelled delicious, and she felt guilty enjoying this fare while Ruckus was probably hungry as hell. MREs couldn't hold a candle to real food.

She scooped some into her mouth and made a soft sound. His glittering black eyes matched his hair, and the uneasiness spread as he watched her eat. He'd set his weapon against the side of the tent but still had a sidearm at his hip. He broke off a hunk of bread and gave it to her. Someone handed her a cup of hot, dark coffee.

"Now, tell me, what has happened to you? Where is your crew?"

She sipped, and the flavor of the rich beans exploded on her tongue. "There was a terrible storm, and we got separated. I've been wandering and am sure glad I found you."

He nodded. She polished off the last of her dinner and popped the remaining bite of bread in her mouth. She glanced at the boats again, and he didn't miss the look.

"I would be so ever grateful if you could...lend me a boat

so that I could get to Yaviza. I'm sure my crew is very worried about me."

"I'm afraid that would be out of the question," he said in a quiet, flat tone. Her stomach dropped, and her heart stalled. He smiled, then said, "I couldn't possibly let a beautiful, lone woman, one who is under FARC's protection, go on such a journey on her own. You will stay here tonight, and we'll get a start in the morning."

"Oh, no. I couldn't impose on you to take me that far. I'm sure I can make my way there. I'm very capable." She rose and wiped her hands on her pants. Backing up toward the boats, she gave him a smile. He didn't return it this time, and a finger of fear went down her spine. Something was different here, something that she couldn't quite grasp.

He rose as she turned and walked toward the boats at a quick pace. Her gasp was audible in the quiet of the jungle. Bodies. Several in the water, more on the bank. FARC uniforms. Her breathing accelerated to labored gasps as she closed her eyes. That's what was different. Escobar wasn't wearing a uniform anymore.

Ruckus had been right, and she should have listened to him. This place had no rules. None whatsoever, no decency, no quarter, no mercy. She was in serious trouble.

He grasped her shoulder. "I'm afraid there's been a change of plans," he said as she looked from the boats to the bodies. Each of the *piraguas* were filled with crates, and she had no doubt about what was in them. Cocaine.

But that's not what chilled her to the bone. She hadn't considered one-way Salazar would fill his ranks. Bribery.

"I'm no longer with FARC. You see, their power is waning, and Salazar pays much better. And word is he wants you, Dana. Where's the man you escaped with?" He used her first name as if they were familiar, intimate. She whirled and stepped back. The rush of alarm was so intense that for an instant she thought her heart would stop altogether.

"He's dead," she said, keeping her focus on Escobar and off the jungle behind him. She didn't have to feign fear. The images of the dead faces were burned into her eyes.

His hand slipped down her arm, and her heart jammed into her ribs, hammering frantically as fear churned through her. "He said he wanted you alive, but he didn't say in what shape," he murmured.

In that moment, she realized there were worse things than death. Much worse. He grabbed her around the waist, grinding his pelvis against hers, the bulge there requiring no explanation what he was going to take from her, panic and revulsion compressing her lungs. With a wave of anger surging through her, she desperately shoved at his chest, bringing up her knee, which glanced off his thigh, but she did some damage. He grunted in pain and then backhanded her across the face.

Pain exploding in her cheek, she reeled away, but he was on her again and she heard some of the men in the compound laugh. Oh, God. He was going to do it right here. Out in the open. She could taste blood in her mouth. Dazed, she tried to push him off her again when he abruptly froze as something wet and sticky splattered all over her.

Escobar collapsed, and she had enough presence of mind to realize that Ruckus had made his move. All around the camp, men where reaching for their weapons. Dana dropped and took cover around the back of one of the canoes. She could hear the constant retort of the suppressed automatic he carried.

There were sounds of running feet, grunts of pain, shouting, then everything was quiet. Shaking like crazy, she looked over the edge of the boat and saw him. He strode through the bodies littering the ground, calmly using his sidearm and putting a headshot into each one of them. Each time the gun went off, she flinched at the sound the barrel should have made, but instead with the suppression, it was just barely audible.

Armed conflict wasn't new to her. She'd seen plenty in her days working as a freelance correspondent with some killings even more brutal than what she'd just seen. She'd been in danger and seen people die, but she'd never been the target of any attack. She'd only reported it. She wasn't stupid. She knew what a SEAL did, that they were trained to outgun, outthink, outrun, and outdo anyone or anything. But seeing Ruckus in action with a steadiness that unnerved her all the way down to the pit of her stomach made her mind just simply cut off and drift. Feeling a bit dazed, she brought her gaze to his. She saw his mouth move, saw his short nod, and then he sent her a message loud and clear. *I got you.*

Boy, did he ever.

Still shaking in the aftermath of her adrenaline rush, she pressed her back against the rough boat and took shallow breaths. She had been so wrong here. Granted, she'd decided his plan was a better one, but caught out in the jungle, there was nowhere for her to go without being hunted again. She also couldn't blow his cover. Now, even though this had all happened, she was sure glad she hadn't.

Escobar had defected to the CLP, and Salazar knew she was gone. He had a ransom on her head, and she had to wonder if she'd even be safe in the US. She was guessing the answer to that question was a resounding no.

"We're getting out of here," he growled. She hadn't known him long, but there was one thing she knew about this man. He was often scowling. That wasn't the case now. Now? He was furious, and it struck her deep in her core. Then it was as if he got a good look at her and he grabbed her arm. "Are you hurt?" His voice was low, hard, and it scared her almost as much as the look on his face.

She couldn't speak. She was so tied up in knots. He gave her a quick shake, looking like he wanted to shake her harder, looking like he wanted to say more, looking like he wanted to break something.

It wouldn't be her. She was made of stronger stuff.

"Are you hurt, Dana?" he asked, and the sound of her name on his lips made everything in her just twirl even harder. She shook her head.

He gave her a quick visual and ran his hands over her body. Now her breath was trapped. He started chucking crates out of the closest canoe, and one of them broke, spilling kilos of white powder on the ground. He didn't even bother to look. Then he picked her up and set her into the boat and pushed it off, jumping inside. He grabbed a paddle and propelled them into the center of the fast-moving river. He started the motor and guided them along.

After a few moments, he reached into his tech vest and pulled out a packet, then ripped it with his teeth. It was one of the moist towelettes that had come with their MREs. He started wiping gently at her face. At first, it didn't register, then she realized. Blood spatter from Escobar.

"I'm sorry."

He didn't say anything, just kept cleaning her face. She grabbed his wrist and he looked at her.

"I was going to go with your suggestion and then that guy busted up that plan."

A muscle jerked in his jaw, his hot gaze drilling into her. "Next time, no discussion. We do it my way."

"Agreed. We do it your way."

It was as if those few words uncorked his temper, and anger flared in his eyes, the muscles of his neck suddenly taut. "This isn't a damn committee, cupcake. I lead, you follow. Clear?"

"Yes, dammit. Clear. You've got the muscle and the guns. I'm along for the ride." She bit her lip. "Can I say that I'm supremely glad that you saved me. A badass with mad warrior skills is exactly what I needed."

"If you let go of my wrist, I'll take care of the rest of this."

She heaved a sigh. His skin was so warm beneath her palm. She didn't want to let go of him. He was solid, and the incident with Escobar was still fresh. She was probably in shock. She drew in a slow, deep breath, tamping down her emotions, drawing up some strength, focusing on how her mother would have handled this. She had always been so strong, up until the end.

Grief hit her hard, but she muscled it back. She had missed being there for her mom because she was off on an assignment. She had missed hugging her mom one last time, telling her she loved her. She regretted it every moment of every day.

She let go of him and he cleaned the rest of her face, moving down to her neck. Dana wished she could get in a shower and scrub herself clean. She could still taste her own blood and smell the metallic scent of Escobar's all over her.

He motored on, and she anxiously watched the water behind them for any signs of pursuit. Finally, as the night deepened, he steered the boat to shore, pulling it up on the bank and covering it in brush. The night was comfortably warm, fragrant with the scent of some kind of wild flower. She spied some white flowers in among the dark green leaves. For a moment, she could almost make believe she was home in San Diego with the bougainvillea vines climbing up the side of her house in the back, reclining in her comfortable lounge chair with a cool drink in her hand. But in the morning, the humidity would return with the sun like a wet woolen blanket.

He touched her shoulder, and she flinched, jumping. "Why don't you change?" he suggested, low and strained. "Then we'll get some sleep."

The remembered feel of Escobar's hands and his body made her skin crawl. She pulled off her pack and dug inside for a clean shirt. She unbuttoned the one she had on and threw it on the ground. She would never wear it again. Pulling the fresh one over her head, she enjoyed the feel of the cool, dry fabric as it settled against her sticky skin.

She wrapped her arms around herself, trying with all her might to calm her racing heart. Much as she hated to admit it, she was feeling weak. She loathed feeling powerless. Coming unhinged out here wouldn't be good for her or for her escort. He looked worried.

"Here, let me show you something simple." She stared at him and nodded, the compassionate look in his eyes making her insides go a little liquid. "Grab my thumb and bend it back." When she did, he went to his knees. "Leaves me vulnerable. Now's the time for that kick to the balls."

She let go of him and stepped back. He bent down and retrieved her shirt, but instead of saying anything, his gaze narrowed and the angle of his jaw hardened. He just dug a hole and buried it without comment.

5

In a jumble of fear and regret, the dream nothing but dark shadows and even frightening meanings, she came suddenly awake. There was a hand over her mouth. Her instincts kicked in, and she tried to fight, but whoever had her only tightened the hold, a big body straddling hers. She gulped down panic and blind terror; striking the person was like hitting granite. Trapped in the remnants of the nightmare, the air heaved in and out of her lungs in tremendous hot, ragged gasps.

Then he spoke into her ear, his voice husky and soft. "It's me, cupcake. Hang on. We have company."

She stilled immediately, her heart pounding, the tentacles of fear leaving her cold and shaking. They were currently well concealed in the jungle, forgoing the comfort of the tent. Ruckus was a master at hiding himself and her. What had he called it? SERE? This would be the evading part, just as he'd done with boosting her up into that tree. Boldly sitting there while the enemy moved right beneath them. It made her heart pound thinking about it.

His attention shifted from her to the direction of the water.

Foliage was above her, the canopy thick and blocking out most of the moonlight, but the water reflected the pale, now-you-see-it-now-you-don't moon off the shimmering surface.

She could just make out his devastating features, his whole body on alert and ready for action. She had to wonder if he was always like this, even when he was home. The training of an elite operative ingrained into him.

She didn't relax until he did. He removed his hand from her mouth. "Armed men. Not sure if it was FARC or CLP," he whispered. "They looked like they were searching."

"Great, we have more people after us."

"If we'd stolen the boat..." He trailed off, and she suddenly realized that Ruckus was still straddling her.

"Right, and we didn't kill CLP drug runners and throw their coke in the dirt. But, nothing stopping them from coming after their stolen boat, too."

"I'll concede that, babe," he said softly.

"Oh, my God. Did you just agree with me? This must be a first."

"I'm not sure that trend will continue," he said wryly. Then he smiled and her world tilted. Dana had been in the company of many men, through many situations, but this one with Ruckus was the strangest. They were together by circumstance and necessity. Strangers, really. Except he'd put his life on the line many times in the past two days. She wasn't sure he even liked her. But with each passing minute, she was getting a handle on him. He might act all tough and pushy, but there was something there, below the surface, like a shiny object beckoning to her. Along with that, there was pain, enough to shadow his eyes.

But what the hell did she know about warriors?

Not much. But *this* warrior. She wanted to know more.

"You okay?" he asked, the smile fading as he searched her eyes.

Her insides jumped. Keep everything inside, keep everything neutral was her mantra. Reporters were objective, even about their own feelings and hang-ups.

"Yes. I'm fine," she responded, meeting his gaze.

"You were having a nightmare. I didn't mean to scare you even more."

"I eat panic for breakfast," she said flippantly, but Ruckus's eyes only sharpened.

"That's a nice canned response, but processing everything that happened yesterday takes time."

She blew out a breath. "I suspect you know something about that."

His mouth skewed wryly again. "Yeah, a bit." He supported himself on his elbows. "We should be quiet and not move until we're sure they don't come back this way." She nodded and his eyes riveted to hers. "For the record, you are one tough little wildcat."

"A wildcat cupcake, huh?"

He chuckled. "Yeah. Not so light and airy. Those sprinkles can be used as lethal weapons."

"You saved me. I was just giving Escobar a piece of my mind with my fists." She caressed his face with her eyes, settling inexplicably on his mouth, that tantalizing mouth. She should really stop looking at it and him. Now. Right now.

She should feel uncomfortable, especially after yesterday and what had happened with Escobar, but she didn't. All the danger wrapped around fleeing for her life seemed to settle in her gut, only upping the tension. She just couldn't get past the fact that he was so willing to be there for her, through anything. Risking his life to save hers, even with the odds so stacked against her.

His big body was intimately joined with hers, his chest pressed against her breasts. She looked up at him, the air between them tightened and heated. He was so close, and he smelled so warm and earthy. Suddenly Dana felt very fragile and very shaky inside. She closed her eyes, clenching her jaw against her own emotions.

Everything tingled in her from her skin to her mind to her fingertips. Her numbness had been safe without letting in emotions, and now with Ruckus, nothing seemed safe.

And she knew that she could never go back to Jeff. That it was over between them. Had been over for some time. He had been part of her life that she'd numbed, and Ruckus made her feel much too alive to lie to herself anymore.

For so long she'd been getting by after her mom's death, trying with all her might to live up to her mother's expectations, fulfill her last wish. Keeping her objectivity in place had gotten her through each waking moment. Her life had been so full of movement and harsh environments. Condemnation and guilt. She opened her eyes. But now her world was filled with this man for the long haul. Because with the danger came her determination to beat the odds, get to Salazar, and kick that bully's ass. She was getting her memory cards back.

"What just happened there?" he asked, his voice dropping an octave, his blue eyes glittering in the eerie silvery light that broke through the canopy, casting his features in stark relief and making her melt inside like warm chocolate. His concern for her was evident.

"I'm not giving up. No matter what happens. I can't."

"Why?"

Suddenly she was close to tears. Her throat tightened.

She blinked several times to push back the overwhelming grief, the ache spreading until she ruthlessly pulled it back. "Because I promised my mom I would do this for her. It's the only thing that's kept me going since she...died."

His blue eyes softened even more. "You were close?" His voice was tentative as if he didn't understand that closeness or understood it too well. She wondered which it was.

"Very." She felt as if every nerve in her body was stretched to the limit, the knot in her stomach sitting like a rock. "Dr. Meredith Sorenson. My dad called her Merry, and she was full of life and so happy most of the time. She was strong, capable, and loved both of us with all that she had. She worked with Doctors Without Borders most of her career, with a brief break here and there to have and raise me. She was this amazing person, selfless, giving, inexhaustible. She cared so much. I miss her so much." Her mother's work had affected her deeply. Dana saw how it had twisted her up and made her even more desperate to ease that suffering. Dana's objectivity was her armor. Without it she was just as exposed to the turmoil her mother endured up until the end.

"I'm sorry." His response was genuine in his voice and features. She trembled slightly as the heat from his body drifted over her skin. She caught a breath in her throat as he lifted a hand to push a lock of hair out of her right eye.

It wasn't that he was being sweet and his response full of his condolences, it was that this hard-edged man could bend enough to give her some comfort. If she melted any more, she would be nothing but liquid.

"I think we're going to have to hoof it. With the river full of the CLP, it's not going to be safe to travel by water."

She sighed. "This is my fault."

"It was a goat fuck and sometimes those can't be helped. Best laid plans and all."

"Goat fuck?"

"It's military slang for something that has gone completely wrong and is unlikely to end positively. Others I will probably use are FUBAR: Fucked up Beyond All Recognition. Then there's cluster fuck, which is something along the lines of goat fuck, but including many more screwed up things. Also SNAFU—Situation Normal, All Fucked Up."

"You sure do have a lot of sayings when something goes wrong. Should I still have faith in the military?"

He chuckled. "We don't complain when it happens. We adapt, but as SEALs we're well aware that a plan only means, in theory, we know what we want to have happen. In reality? When the bullets start flying, that tends to distract us from any type of preconceived notion. It happens to any battle-hardened team. We have to address the immediate threat, then quickly, as much as possible, get back to the plan. There is only one guarantee. Someone will be shooting at us."

"Oh, like you did when you found me, half naked in Salazar's house. What did you think? I was his whore?"

"It crossed my mind once I could get it back on track."

"So, even with the mess behind us, we are now back on the plan?"

"Yes, ma'am," he said, but his voice was softer, and it sent shivers over her skin.

"Thank you, by the way. I'm so grateful you were there."

"I did what needed to be done. I told you, they didn't worry me, and there was no way I was going to let that bastard put his hands on you ever again. He got what he deserved. He wasn't taking you back as a hostage. No freaking way." The anger in his voice made her heart turn over. Without thinking, she lifted her head and pressed a kiss to his scratchy cheek. The tension climbed a notch, radiating like a force field around them. His expression altered as if he'd just found something infinitely precious. Dana's heart started stammering, and suddenly it was impossible to breathe. He stared at her for a moment, this hot, sexy man, then he brought his mouth into full contact with hers.

The kiss was slow, soft, and so unbelievably gentle that it left her absolutely breathless, and her whole body so in tune with his. A sudden urgency sizzled through her, and she locked her arms around him.

TOO MANY MILES AWAY, sitting on a rise, surveying the forest in a back and forth vigil, Kid Chaos listened unabashedly to everything Ruckus said to the beautiful Dana. His LT was putting the moves on her, and that was turning him on.

Back at the stronghold, *of course* he hadn't wanted to go downstairs and help Scarecrow. He'd wanted to stay upstairs and save the babe. Not that he would ever cheat. It was his one hard and fast rule. No cheating. It hurt like hell. He should know.

He rubbed at his breastbone at a place where a stick was poking him. That wasn't emotion, he assured himself. He was long over it. No, that feeling was just a stick stuck in his craw.

He had been all about rescue, Boy Scout stuff and, well, he wasn't fucking blind. She was a beautiful woman wrapped up in terry cloth, and he was a red-blooded male. So, hell yes, he was going to look.

Looked like LT was taking orders from his dick. And that was one powerful admiral.

He heard a soft groan, a woman's groan, and his imagination started filling in all sorts of pieces whether he wanted it to or not.

This was torture.

A long-distance, voyeuristic ménage à trois—except, fuck it, he was getting hard.

There was nothing but rapid breaths, hot breathing over the mic, and he saw Cowboy lift his head and their eyes met. Kid grinned and Cowboy returned it. He mouthed *What the fuck?* Kid blew him a kiss, and Cowboy gave him the finger. He shook his head and got up, probably to relieve himself.

The other guys were stirring, and with the looks between them and their wide grins, they were aware of what was happening.

He hadn't listened on purpose. Ruckus must have keyed his mic by accident. But in the dark before the dawn, Kid missed his current girlfriend, Mia. She was all soft and sweet, the total opposite of his lean, badass self.

His appetites were just as powerful as his predilection for a healthy dose of adrenaline every day. There was nothing more satisfying than having a woman all over him, submitting to his control as he made sure she was screaming and begging for more with that breathless quality in her voice he couldn't get enough of, and sliding his aching dick into her, slick and ready for him was the best damn thing.

Damn he missed Mia.

He knew he was a lot to take, but that was too damn bad if it was too much. He wasn't apologetic about who he was. He played hard and fought even harder. Adrenaline junkie about covered it. He was most in his element when he was in a firefight, HALO free-falling, or hang-gliding off a cliff in

Peru. It was all about challenging the elements, gravity, physics, death. Sniping was his specialty, and although he valued human life, taking an enemy's was his job and he never hesitated when he had someone in his scope. The critical talent was his willingness to look a man in the eyes and headshot him without flinching. He was not just chaos personified, but a cold perfect zero as well, a term that meant one shot, one kill. He'd been trained well by Uncle Sam, and he used every *damn* thing he'd learned while in "his" service. It just happened he got the bonus of defending the United States. That and the honor of serving on the teams made him a dangerous SEAL. Just what the red, white, and blue ordered.

Since LT keyed his mic, all the guys could hear him, but it was clear they took it in stride and went back to sleep, snores all the way around. Well, except for him. He was the one on guard duty.

"Ruckus?" she said, her voice breathless, and Kid wanted to groan out loud.

"Yeah?" LT wasn't in any better shape. Kid had never heard that tone come over the radio.

"Is the danger past?"

"I think so."

Not by a long-shot, Kid thought. He had Scarecrow's satellite computer, and they were monitoring the area around Ruckus. When he spied all the red dots moving steadily toward them, he had to break radio silence. Damn, the boss was going to have his ass when he realized he'd been putting on a show for seven guys and Kid hadn't said a word.

∼

"Uh, LT?"

With his lips still on the cupcake's soft and delectable mouth, the sound buzzing in his ears didn't register. She brushed her lips over his, and he lost focus again, opening his mouth over hers, plunging deeply, taking her into him. Holy hell, she was eating him alive, her tongue thrusting between his lips and unhinging him in seconds. He was trapped, his dick going stone hard, his shoulders pulling tight as he tasted her. Savored her. The woman was one tasty morsel.

"Earth to LT." Ruckus froze as Kid's urgent tone broke through his sensual haze. He was furious with himself for his lack of control. But then he looked down into those dazed, stirred-up honey brown eyes, and the connection that had been sizzling between them coalesced into something more. That's when it hit him—the loneliness had been with him for as long as he could remember, even through the train wreck of his marriage. He had a bond with the men he fought with, socialized with them even when they weren't on duty, but even those friendships weren't a substitute for female companionship.

The more he looked into those eyes, the more alone he felt, a huge hollowness in the middle of his chest. She could fill it. Her vibrancy, the life in her—he wanted that, craved it. But he dismissed that thought. His track record with women was so abysmal, he'd be a fool to even take the risk of getting hurt again.

"LT." Kid's voice intensified.

"What?" He went to key his mic and swore a blue streak in his head. It had been open. All this time. Damn.

"Yeah."

He pushed his aroused, protesting body off hers and stood. Her sultry eyes tracked him as he moved away from her. Lowering his voice, pinching the bridge of his nose between his fingers, he ground out, "Were you listening this whole time?"

"Yeah, you must have keyed your mic by mistake. I was getting bored as hell, and with all due respect, that was hot... sir." He made kissing noises.

"Kid?" Ruckus growled.

"Yeah?" Kid said as if he didn't have a care in the world.

"Remind me to kick your ass the next time I see you," Ruckus said gruffly.

"Copy that, LT," Kid said cheerily.

He waited impatiently, fuming. "I'm assuming you contacted me for a reason?"

"Yes, sir. If you're quite done with the kissy face, I thought you'd want to know there's a large group of tangos moving your way."

Ruckus sighed, gritting his teeth. "Let me guess. From the north."

"Yeah, you get the Cracker Jack prize and from the South on the river. If you stay at your present location, you're going to get boxed in. They're cutting off egress. You're going to have to cross the river to avoid them. It's clear on the other side."

"Copy that," he growled.

"Oh, and LT?"

"Yes, Kid." He said it like he wanted to grind up the little bastard into hamburger.

"Next time, make sure your mic volume is turned up. I loved the entertainment."

"Kid..."

"Hey? Is that asking too much?"

He was going to open some chaos on that kid's ass. He didn't even bother to answer, just closed communications. He walked over to Dana, his face grim. "We've got a whole lot of company, and you're not going to like my plan, babe. Grab your pack, and let's go."

She groaned. "What is it?"

"We're going swimming with the gators."

"I don't want to be on the menu," she protested. But he grabbed her arm and led her down to the water's edge.

"That's not the worst of it." He looked at her.

Her brows rose, and she rubbed at her forehead. "There's more good news?"

"Yeah, we're going to have to cross back."

"You're just full of glad tidings. I so love camping with you."

He flashed her a grin. "Grab on to my vest and don't let go for anything. Take a breath."

She took her breath and he took his.

Before he dragged her under with him, she gave him a sidelong glance. "Is this what you call a cluster?"

"The fuckiest of all clusters."

6

The water was a lot cooler than the air and felt good against his skin. The pack dragged at his shoulders but didn't slow his swimming. He could handle the strong current. The crossing didn't take long.

They hit the far bank as the sound of a motor broke the early dawn. He dragged Dana with him into the dense overgrowth. She was gasping, but he was barely breathing hard. He watched the boat pass slowly as if they were looking for something, but again, he was much too good at concealment. They didn't detect the boat. But the guys on land, whoever they were, would stumble across it and then they'd be looking for them.

"Let's never do that again. This side of the river is so nice."

He led her through the jungle once again and chuckled. "It's exactly the same scenery, but nice try."

As they got deeper, the first drops started to fall. "At least we're already wet," she muttered, but trudged steadily behind him.

He liked that she could keep up with him even at a

punishing pace. She had mentioned she was a runner. Her choice of exercise had come in handy in the Gap.

"Darwin wasn't full of shit," she said, "It really is survival of the fittest." Thunder rumbled in the distance, lightning shimmering in the haze. The wet vapor of the rain forest smothered down around them, the river to their left, dense jungle to their right.

Ruckus was compromised—by her voice, by those serious brown eyes penetrating any wall he put between them. She was damn bound and determined to get those memory cards back, and he suspected her motivations were more personal than maybe she even realized. Not a good combination, going in blindly after a goal fueled by emotions. She didn't know that he had other plans for her, plans that wouldn't end pretty. It almost hurt to know that she'd feel deeply betrayed, and he couldn't seem to find that detachment he needed. But those were the drawbacks of being in command. "You holding up okay, cupcake?"

"Yes, sir, LT."

He chuckled softly, his vigilance honed as his affection for his unexpected package deepened but hampered by the sounds of the incoming storm as thunder moved closer.

Yes, she was something else. Even with the dawn, there was a gray quality to the jungle as the overcast sky blocked out all attempts of the sun to break through. In the unnatural dusk, rain made a hissing sound against the leaves as the first drops of the promised storm hit them. Then it was a deluge, an ocean of water pouring out of the sky as the storm settled just above them. Sheets of water made it almost impossible to see even a few feet in front of them.

～

IT WAS GOING to be a day of double-time humping, preparing to close the gap between their leader and them. Kid was still getting amusement out of LT's uncharacteristic break in SEAL protocol and locking lips with the terry cloth babe. He and the rest of the team were breaking camp when Scarecrow shouted, "Fuck! Tangos moving in. Kid!"

Kid dropped everything and raced over to the computer. He keyed his mic. "LT! Bug out! Bug out! Tangos coming at you from the right. Move!"

But even as he looked at the computer Scarecrow held, his breath trapped in his chest, the blue blip didn't move.

Then the sound of thunder from miles away rumbled like a waking beast, and Kid's stricken eyes met Scarecrow's. "He can't hear me." He and the pretty reporter were cut off and on their own with three groups of red dots surrounding them.

"LT..." Static interrupted Kid's voice. "...tangos..." Then it was gone, nothing but white noise. The heavy rain was blocking out his transmission. Ruckus immediately stopped moving and looked around. He wasn't sure which tangos Kid had been referring to—the ones coming upriver or the ones across the river. He made the decision to head right, deeper into the forest. Moving blindly, the rain hampering their movement, they crashed through the overgrowth, beneath the canopy of huge trees. Mercifully, the rain started to abate as the storm moved off. The pattering of rain slowed as the saturated jungle tried to absorb even more water.

He paused and listened, all his senses alert. The sound of gunfire burst in the silence, rapid and close. He jerked a look in the direction. To his right! That's what Kid had been warning him about. Assault rifles. More FARC? CLP? Pana-manian troops, or a drug deal gone bad?

A second later he was grabbing her hand and pulling her back toward the river. Caught between the CLP, FARC, and drug runners was a trifecta of death, and the river was their only hope. Crossing back over would put them behind the advancing tangos on the opposite bank, conceal them from the boat searching for them, and get them away from this immediate threat.

Baddies were all over the area. He sensed them, spreading out in the jungle, raking through it. He suspected they would shoot first and ask questions later. That was his locked and loaded plan of action.

As soon as they made the shore, he looked down the river and sure enough, the boat was on the shore. Looked like the CLP and another set of armed aggressors were going at it. He waded in and said, "Hold on!" before he took them both under, swimming as fast as he could with both his pack and Dana's weight. He was across three-quarters of the way when he surfaced for a quick look. Off to his right, he spied them, two big, mother-f-ing caimans. They splashed into the water with their huge tails thrashing.

He had no intention either one of them would become gator food.

Doubling his efforts, he was almost to shore when he saw them swimming strongly toward him and Dana. He propelled her with all his might forward, and she shot through the water, and God bless that beauty, she continued to swim.

He dropped his pack and reached for his knife as the first beast, maw gaping, came for him. He avoided the jaws with a powerful push below. As soon as the animal was above him, he rose and jabbed in with his knife, piercing the soft underbelly, and opened him up tail to jaw. Then he swam like hell. He bulleted through the water, but just as he was almost to shore, something powerful clamped onto his boot. The minute the caiman had him, it started turning into its death spiral to pull off a chunk of Ruckus, dragging him deeper.

∾

BREATHING HARD, Dana watched the water with frantic eyes. Ruckus hadn't surfaced, and she realized why. Gators. She saw their scaly backs as they briefly glazed the top of the water, then disappeared. The gunfire was loud behind her, but all her focus was on the churning water. When she saw the blood, she made a soft, distressed sound. The waiting crushing her. He surfaced, and he and the gator rolled around, a knife flashing. Then they were gone again. Her breath trapped in her lungs as the water settled.

She picked up a stick and was about to head into the water when a cold voice said in Spanish, "Don't move. Drop it."

She did as she was told and put up her hands. Just then, a mountain of power exploded from the surface, water sluicing off him, his semi-automatic in his hands as he opened fire, his face contorted into a savage mask, driven into survival mode, all his instincts active. She dove for cover as he took out whoever was behind her. After the sound of automatic fire ended, her face in the sand and her body drenched in sweat and river water, she pushed up, every inch of her aching. He really was the only thing that stood between her and death or something much worse. She'd known that somewhere in the back of her mind, but everything rested on his broad, capable shoulders. Her heart lurched in her chest, something shifting, settling, taking hold of her just like his mouth had this morning when he'd kissed her. God help her, she wanted more. With that came guilt and anticipation.

The next thing she knew, he literally jerked her to her feet and pulled her with him at a breakneck pace, away from the bodies, the river, armed combatants, and freaking gators. My God, he'd literally wrestled alligators for her. She held onto his hand like a lifeline. Rain started to fall again, closing her and this ruthless-eyed warrior behind a curtain of gray as the jungle swallowed them whole.

They ran for an hour, straight out, no slowing, but lack of sleep, food, and water were getting to her. She stumbled, and Ruckus slowed, catching her in his arms. They took cover behind a tree, and just like the first night she'd met him, he covered her body with his. The rain had washed the mud and sweat off them as it continued to fall. He was still vigilant, his wide chest heaving, he'd taken off his uniform shirt and was now in nothing but the green T-shirt and tech vest. His eyes scanned, and all she could feel was supreme relief that he was alive, that he had the kind of skills that transitioned to just about anything from armed combat to swimming swift currents to tangling with territorial marine life with very sharp teeth.

In the midst of all this danger, she'd never felt safer in her life.

"I think we're in the clear," he said, his voice low and husky. All she could do was look up at him helplessly. When she didn't answer, he glanced at her, then back to the forest, but there must have been something in her eyes because his intense gaze went back to hers.

Wordlessly they stared at each other. She was unexpectedly close to tears, so aware of him as a man, as if her body had a million little sensors in it and he tripped every one of them. It was as if he'd reached out and touched her, caressing her in the most intimate way. She flattened both hands against the hard muscles of his chest. What passed between them was definitely all about the man/woman connection as the intimacy grew and out-steamed the jungle around them.

His blue eyes created a dizzying effect, and his wordless stare said he was just as aware of her as a woman, the savage light there making her body soften and ache. He touched her face, a familiar, intimate, protective touch. She closed her eyes and leaned into that light pressure. He made a deep, satisfied male sound in the back of his throat at her reaction.

Was this his protective and amazing warrior instincts setting off a primal reaction in her? She was too jazzed by him to even sort that out. Jeff wasn't someone she had to consider in this; not even the physical with him was as potent as Ruckus's hand against her face. Her hands traveled up to his shoulders, roped with muscle, to the back of his neck and up into his hair, her arms twining around his neck.

Feeling totally shredded inside, she wrestled with her conscience and her burgeoning desire, the awful unsatisfied ache throbbing through her whole body. When his chest pressed against her sensitized nipples, she cried out.

Her eyes popped open when he crushed her in a hard, fierce embrace, his hand roughly tangling in her loose hair as he jammed her head against him.

Immobilized by the onslaught of need, Dana clung to him, certain she would collapse if he let her go. She had never experienced anything like it—the heavy, surging feeling of two parts merging, the awesome power of two strong personalities meshing, the stunning wash of wanting. It had been a lifetime of not knowing what it really meant to be alive. And now it was all out of control, the need, the hunger, the raw emotion. But even so, not enough. Never enough.

Her breathing frantic, she needed him, needed more. Locking her arms around him, she pulled herself flush against him, giving into the need.

Hoarsely whispering her name, he grasped her hair and tilted her mouth up to his. His heart pounded in tandem with hers. He took her mouth. The surge of raw sexual energy was like being infused with pure lightning.

Her breathing paralyzed, she lifted herself higher and opened her mouth, needing the heat of him. Ruckus shuddered, grinding his mouth against hers as he crushed her even tighter. Full, blunt-force body contact.

Everything she had ever believed about herself was incinerated by that hot, wet, plundering kiss. Making a low sound of restraint, he tried to tear his mouth away, but she grasped his face, holding him to her, unable to let him go. She had to finish this, had to have him or she would break into thousands of frantic bits.

His breathing raw and labored, Ruckus ripped his mouth away and framed her face with his hands, "Dana, we can't. I don't have anything..."

"It's okay," she pleaded with him, her voice breaking. "Birth control."

She took his hand and ran it down her body to the waistband of her pants. Another tremor shuddered through him when he released the snap, his other hand cupping her breast, kneading and rubbing his thumb over her nipple. "Fuck, cupcake," he whispered brokenly, his breath hot against her ear.

She bit her lip as his big, hot hand slipped between her clothes and skin. Desperate for him, she cupped the hard ridge bulging beneath the placket of his camo pants, and he clutched her and stiffened, his body rigid with tension. She moved again, and he clutched her tighter, then his hand pushed against her pelvis, his fingers finding her core, moist and hot. He teased his fingers over her again and again while she fondled any part of him she could, her hand going up to the stubble on his face, the scratch of it against her palm turning her on even more.

Bracing her weight, he thrust his fingers up inside her, his mouth taking her low cry of satisfaction at the penetration. She ached for his hard cock.

Then his thumb was pressing on her in quick circles and her world splintered as she came in a hard, blinding rush.

He fumbled with his pants, and Dana cried out when he pulled them down, crying out again when she felt him free and hard. He stripped her pants and underwear off her in one quick movement. Blinded by sensation, she arched, but instead of entering her, he gathered her hands above her head, his fingers locked around her wrists. "I want to fuck you until I feel all your cupcake sweetness clench around my cock." He rubbed against her again, then demanded, "Touch me, Dana. I loved the feel of your small hands all over me." He pressed his face into her neck.

She wrestled out of his grasp and slipped her hand around the length of him. He made such a deliciously deep sound in the back of his throat; she knew she'd never get sick of hearing that over and over. She rubbed the silky, engorged tip with her thumb and Ruckus thrust into her palm, his breathing ragged.

"Feels so good, babe."

She'd never wanted to go down on a man as much as

right this minute, but they were too far gone for that. He tightened his hold around her middle and lifted her almost on her tiptoes.

"Put my dick into you. I want to feel you around me."

She guided him to her, on the brink from just the feel of him, his husky voice. He choked out her name and thrust into her, gathering her butt in his hands.

"Wrap your legs around me." His eyes were dark and as deep and incandescent as a flame.

With her back braced against the tree and thunder rumbling again right over them, he lifted her, and she locked her ankles to the middle of his back.

She opened her eyes and watched his beautiful face contort as he thrust into her, slowly at first, then faster, groaning at their first contact. He looked tough and sexy, the bleeding from a gash on his forehead an angry red line, his tousled hair glittered with moisture that ran off his nose and dripped from his scarred chin.

Thunder rolled through the leaden skies and through them. The rain came a little harder as sensations gathered, centering right on where he was entering her. Every thrust brought her closer and closer, until her body felt as tight as a glove. The thunder overhead and was now trapped inside her. Then everything exploded, and pulses of release ripped through her. A tortured groan wreaked havoc inside her as his hips twisted, his own climax pumping into her.

Incoherent and shattered, she hung on to him, a rock-solid handhold in this raging storm. It seemed like an eternity passed before bits of consciousness returned full force. She had her arms still wrapped around him. He was breathing deeply, supporting her with those heavily muscled arms, the rounded bulge of his bicep filling out the T-shirt's short sleeves.

Trembling and weak, and feeling as if every bone in her body had been liquefied, she folded around him, aware of how tightly he was holding her, aware of how badly he was trembling.

Her face wet from the now diminishing rain, she cupped his head and tightened her legs, an unbearable tenderness welling up in her as she cradled him against her. This had been like spontaneous combustion, and she had to face the fact that what she had with Jeff couldn't even scratch the surface of what she had found with this stranger, this badass warrior. And, unlike Jeff, she wanted to know everything about him. Delve down into his soul and discover all his secrets, the very essence of him.

That thought rocked her, because there was no future here. He was pledged to the military and she spent more time running the globe than Ruckus probably did. Jeff could attest to that.

In hindsight, she should have broken it off with Jeff. It was why the thought of marriage with him had made her palms sweat. He wasn't the man for her.

The fact remained that she and this SEAL had something going on for sure. She had no idea where it would lead, but her sense of adventure was all up for the challenge. The fact that she was having feelings for him was totally natural. He'd saved her life so many times. She rubbed her palm over his soft, wet hair.

Ruckus turned has face against her neck, his hands still supporting her. His voice muffled, he asked, "Are you okay, cupcake?"

Moved beyond words by his concern for her and overcome with her need to be honest with him, she pressed her mouth against his temple. Her own voice was very uneven as she whispered, "You should know. You're the one who literally wrestled freaking alligators for me."

"Technically, they were caiman, a bit smaller."

"Really, you want to split hairs here? They still had some pretty sharp teeth and were eyeing us both for dinner."

He raised his head and gave her a wry smile. Damn, he had impossibly thick lashes. "Is everything an argument with you?"

"It's a healthy debate. Do you have a problem with a woman having an opinion?"

"Nope, as long as she keeps it to herself."

She gasped and smacked him on his very hard shoulder. "Put me down, you caveman."

The muscles in his back bunched, and he wiggled his hips, sending aftershocks through her. "I don't think so. I'm kind of enjoying having you at my mercy."

Her heart tripped over itself then dissolved into a puddle. He gave her an incinerating look that made her want to find a resort, a bed, and many days to delve into all that promise in those dark eyes.

"You really have a caveman complex, don't you?"

He chuckled, and the sound of his amusement moved through her like the desire had only moments before. "I'm interested in pulling your hair, but it has nothing to do with dragging you anywhere except beneath me." With a breathless, mighty move, he caught her underneath her armpits and lifted her as easily as he'd fought those creepy predators. For just a moment, he held her aloft, then he leaned forward and kissed her mouth, taking his time as those powerful arms kept her suspended.

He set her down, and she went to get her pants and underwear, wobbling a bit. He steadied her immediately, then said, "Allow me." He bent at the waist, the quick view of his thick torso, those lean abs and groin much too brief. She'd never wanted to see a man naked as much as she wanted to see him. Completely buck ass naked for hours so she could explore every inch of his hard, muscled body.

He held her delicate panties in those big hands. "Step in, cupcake. We don't have all friggin' day," he growled. She set her hand on his shoulder. God, she loved his grumpiness. She stepped into the panties as he kissed her stomach, his lips soft, his breath warm against her skin. He pressed his face harder, breathing her in, his face scratchy, sending tingling waves out in surges. His tongue licked her ribs, then he bit her gently before pulling the panties up. He released the waistband with a snap, and she laughed.

His face was hard, aroused. "If we weren't out in this jungle with all these bastards after us, a package to pick up, and a mission to complete, I'd have you holed up somewhere for a freaking week."

"Pants," she said with a grin. "We don't have all friggin' day." She mimicked his deep voice, poking fun at him.

He grabbed her around the waist and dragged her against him. "Do me up, first, will ya? If I go back down for those pants, I might just go down on you, my dick will get harder than I already am, and we'll get ourselves shot to death because I'm doing you instead of watching our backs."

The laughter faded from her face at his intense look. Reaching down, her breath trapped in her throat, her eyes never leaving his, she grasped the edge of his underwear and, not meaning to, fondled him as she pulled it up over his hot erection.

"Fuck," he said softly, pressing his forehead to hers, his breathing uneven. "Love those damn hands."

Unable to resist it, she leaned forward and kissed him. Rubbing her lips over his mouth as she found and zipped him up, careful over that tantalizing bulge. Then she did up the button.

Her hands lingered around his lean waist, enjoying his warm skin. "How was that? Did I handle your...uh...hardware satisfactorily?"

With a thick groan in the back of his throat, he crowded her against the tree. God, the man could kiss, putting his whole self into it, leaning in harder, making her mindless with the taste of him, never giving her a chance to catch her breath.

It was like running full out.

He slowed, then broke the kiss, pressing his forehead to hers. Taking a deep breath, he crouched and helped her with her pants, this time keeping his mouth and face away from her torso.

He had something that weakened her. Not so much his looks; she'd been around hundreds of handsome, dangerous men. The way he kissed was a good contender—she was nearly melting at the lingering feel of his lips against hers as they shouldered their packs and started out again. He could touch her in places she didn't want any man to. The vulnerability warned her that connections to him would compromise her. She completely understood why she'd taken up with Jeff. He was no threat. He was easygoing, sweet, and kind. All this time she was just marking time with him because he'd been safe.

Not the same kind of safe that Ruckus was. The SEAL was a challenge, arrogant, pushy, bossy, and amazing. Jeff was no effort. All she could do was feel relief.

That weakness attacked her again, the need to share, to not be so alone. But she couldn't. She had a mission, too, and it wasn't to get lost in Ruckus. She'd promised her mom to do something important, and she couldn't let her down.

Not like she'd done six months ago. She'd failed so utterly in her pledge that guilt, the kind that twisted someone into something unrecognizable, seized her and wouldn't let go. How could she deserve to find any kind of happiness when there was so much suffering in the world? Her mom had given up everything for it.

How could Dana do any less?

7

They didn't walk far. Ruckus stopped and looked around. "This is a good place to make camp. We need rest, food, and sleep."

She nodded. "Do you think this is far enough away?"

"Yeah. We can't even hear gunfire, and those groups are probably more interested in fighting each other. The CLP has their hands full for now."

He pulled out the MREs and that cooking thing he heated them up in, focusing on the packets.

"Do you think what happened back there warrants your name? At least your first name."

He looked up and shrugged. "I guess so." It was a few more moments before he caught her with his blue eyes and said, "It's...Bowie."

She absorbed the power of it, the lethal quality to it. "As in the knife?"

"Yeah," he said, "My old man had a sense of humor."

"Why is that? I think it's sexy, strong, and it suits you."

"He named me after a knife as a joke. He thought I was a weak little bastard."

The anger suffused his face, and his voice held something more than rage; there was bitterness and pain.

"Well, you showed him."

"Yeah, I guess I did, but it doesn't matter. He's dead."

It did matter. She could see that. It mattered immensely. Someone who had that much anger cared a whole hell of a lot. "What about your mom?"

"She's still alive."

That was all he said, as if that was all there was. Nothing more about the woman who had nurtured him, kissed his boo-boos and been there for him when he was sick, made his lunches, helped him with his homework.

He finished preparing the meal and dished out the contents of the packets. She wanted to ask more questions, but she could see that he was at the end of the conversation.

"I need to mention something to you. It probably doesn't matter, but I sorta have a boyfriend."

His head jerked up and there was a quality to his eyes that made her shiver. "Kinda, sorta...what the hell, Dana?"

"It's complicated."

"The hell it is. You should have mentioned him before this."

"Exactly. I should have. But I didn't. At times, I forgot. Your fault."

"My fault? What—"

"You make me forget about any other man. Sue me. I couldn't help it."

His mouth tightened, and he looked away, satisfaction mixing with the annoyance. "We just had a thing, right? I saved your life, and you're a beautiful, dynamic woman. We lost our heads. No biggie."

She shrugged. "Right. Lost ourselves." She looked off

toward the mountains, then back at him. Toying with the meal, she said, "Do you think we can do that again?"

He released a puff of air on a short laugh. "Does this guy know how you feel about him?"

"I think he's going to ask me to marry him."

He pinched the bridge of his nose. "That's pretty deep, Dana."

"I know. I should have been smarter, stronger, and broken it off. But he was comfortable."

"I'm not comfortable, Dana. Far from it."

"I know."

"Just so you're aware. I don't do fluffy and sunny."

"Nope. Got that, Mr. Grumpy."

They finished their meal in silence. He rose and said, "I'm going to find some water and refill our supply, clean the dishes, and bury this stuff." He crouched and pulled the sidearm at his hip out of the holster. "You know how to use this?"

"No. I've never shot a gun."

"Fired, cupcake. It's fired a gun."

"Excuse me. Fired a gun."

He ruffled her hair like she was a five-year-old boy, but it was with obvious affection, so she let it pass. "It's easy. It's ready to fire. Just point at center mass and pull the trigger. There's fifteen rounds in there."

"Rounds are bullets. I know that."

He smiled and said, "Yeah, they're bullets."

He rose and grabbed the M4 and walked away. She set the gun down, uneasy with something that could kill people in her hand. She pulled out her cell, smart enough to get one that was waterproof, so the dunk in the river was nothing. Of course, there was no signal way out here, and reception outside of Turbo had been non-existent. She couldn't call him even if she wanted to and delivering her information to him over the phone didn't sit right with her. She'd have to wait.

Tucking the phone back in her pocket, she set up the tent and slipped inside. It looked like it was going to start raining again.

A few short minutes later, Ruckus...Bowie came into camp, and her stomach jumped at the sight of him. His father might have named him that for a joke, but he was just like that knife: keen-edged, made for combat, and dangerously beautiful. He walked with confidence, his vigilance on him like a mantle. When he crawled into the tent, he seemed to take up all the available space. "Boots and socks," he said, his hand open, fingers waggling in a gimme gesture.

She unlaced them and pulled them off along with her socks. He did the same, and he set them off to the side. "Give them time to dry. We don't want wet feet. Worst possible scenario for blisters that will slow us down."

He looked tired, and that wasn't a stretch. He hadn't slept much the night before and even before daybreak had been forging rivers, tangling with the wildlife, and shooting people. It seemed as if she'd been running forever.

"I'll take the first watch."

"No," she said, adamantly. "I'll take it."

"Everything is a damn argument," he muttered under his breath.

She caught his face between her hands, her thumbs caressing his cheekbones. He looked startled for a minute at both the move and probably the fierce look on her face. "This time, I'm winning. You need rest. You've been through hell and back, mostly because of me. I'm sure you could have evaded, survived....

"Survive, evade—"

"Whatever! SERE'd much more easily without me. You've saved my life several times over, and we shared body fluids. So it gives me the right to argue here."

"I think you were born to argue."

"Maybe. My dad said I have a healthy attitude."

"His nice way of saying you're a little brat."

She smiled. "Probably. I got high marks in high school and college for debate."

"I bet you did. You probably exhausted everyone to death."

"For a stoic, monosyllabic man, you sure do have a lot to complain about."

"I only have one damn thing to complain about, and that's you."

She raised her chin. "Tough. You're stuck with me and my exhaustive personality. So freaking give me that gun and let me guard you for a few hours. I promise I won't tell the SEAL police the big, bad warrior went to sleep on the job."

"Oh, for the love of God, here. Take the pistol. Do you want the M4? You can strap extra mags to your chest and go at it Rambo style."

She did take the handgun like it was a snake. "No, I would probably kill us both using your semi-automatic juggernaut of a weapon, and I would never want to take any Rambo credit away from you." He glared at her, then promptly stretched out and laid his head in her lap. She caught a smirk as he closed his eyes. "Even if you told the SEAL police, I would deny it."

Her amusement tinged her words. "I'm a well-respected reporter. I protect my sources."

"And your bodyguards?"

She couldn't help it. She reached down and ran her

hands through his hair, massaging the back of his neck. "Most definitely and most importantly my bodyguards. I'm not stupid, but I'm greedy. I want to keep all the blood I have inside my body."

"Copy that."

For a few minutes, all she heard were the sounds of the jungle. He sighed heavily and said into the silence, "My last name is Cooper." Then he promptly fell asleep.

Lieutenant Bowie "Ruckus" Cooper. Her throat suddenly tight, she took a steadying breath, searching the jungle from one side to the other. She had to be realistic. This was a temporary situation. It wasn't forever. They were worlds and jobs apart. And yet she couldn't shake the feeling that while being held hostage in the stronghold of a psychopathic egomaniac, she might have found the best thing to ever happen to her in the form of stacked muscles, the most beautiful blue eyes, and a very grumpy disposition.

And maybe a heart of gold?

～

RUCKUS OPENED HIS EYES, instantly awake and aware of his surroundings. Jungle. The Darién freaking Gap. Soft, beautiful woman-pillow.

Dana.

She certainly wasn't one of his SEALs to command. Amen to that. Her arm rested across his chest. He turned his head and saw that her chin was lying on her chest, but her hand was wrapped around the nine-millimeter. Sleeping, but ready for action. He grinned. Damn, she was something. He rose and smoothly slipped the gun out of her slack hold and holstered it. Careful not to wake her, he grasped the nape of her neck and, supporting her shoulder, laid her down. A sigh fell from her lips as her body relaxed against his hands. His gaze lingered on the curve of her face, the long expanse of her throat, the wild tousle of dark tresses brushing his wrist and spreading out on his pack as he eased her onto it. She had a hold on him that half fascinated and half scared the hell out of him. He wanted out of this jungle and the whole Hector Salazar mission behind him. Looking at her stirred his sexual restlessness, something that had been there since he'd seen her in that terry cloth and watched her get dressed, the memory of her toned, smooth back haunting his fitful, frustrating dreams.

His thoughts wandered back to their tree-hugging sex, and immediately he wanted to turn her into his arms, wanted to feel her come awake, wanted to slip hard and hot inside her.

He forced himself to move away from her, his breathing uneven. Ruckus ducked out of the tent knowing he couldn't stay there beside her and not touch her.

R&R with her—them one-on-one for days—took over his thoughts instead. Maybe by then he could figure out what was happening between the two of them. He nixed that idea. Who was he kidding? He wasn't relationship material. Sex was what was happening between the two of them and definitely a friendship, albeit a contrary one. How could it ever be anything else with this cupcake?

He was welded to the team, their leader. Someone had to keep those knuckleheads in line. He would give his all to them with nothing left over for anyone else. He already knew he wasn't husband material. Mary Jo had reminded him of that every day they were married and well after the divorce had been final. He couldn't give her what she wanted. Her requests had gone beyond who he thought he could be, and it scared the hell out of him. He wasn't proud of it, but his resistance was engraved on the scars he kept hidden.

Just like he hadn't been son material. His old man had used his punishing words and fists to make sure he understood that, but the icing on that shit cake had been his mom. He'd only wanted to protect her, but the minute he'd knocked his bastard of a father out cold, she'd forced him to leave. Kicked him out of the house and told him never to come back.

And he hadn't. No matter how hard those first few weeks were, trying to survive and finish high school, then all the SEAL tests, both the physical and mental before he could even go on to basic training at Great Lakes. Then onto Coronado, California, and the massive Naval Air Base where he'd really started the work of becoming a SEAL—Basic Underwater Demolition/SEAL Training, a grueling twenty-four-week course with one week deemed as Hell for a reason.

But Ruckus had taken it on like a ravenous wolf, excelled, graduated. During his twenty years, he'd taken college courses, gotten his college degree, been recommended by his CO to Officer Candidate School, and earned his bars. The one thing he was sure of in his life was that he *was* SEAL material.

His mom had tried to reach out to him once he'd received news that his mean drunk of a father had died in a bar brawl, but he'd ignored her, never even went to the funeral, nursing his bitterness like his own child.

He did some calisthenics to warm up and wake up his muscles. He was tired, but his conditioned muscles didn't even twinge. Stripping to the waist, he poured some water into one of the dishes and dipped in a cloth. Once again using Dana's soap, he washed his body.

He swallowed his bitterness, a bit testy that Dana had reminded him of his failures by asking about his family and background. It wasn't her fault. Whether it was her interviewing skills, his weakness for her, or her mesmerizing personality, he felt his barriers slipping, and that wasn't good. Not for her and not for him. Letting that rage surface after he'd worked so hard to keep it in check wasn't healthy for him.

It was mid-day, about three hours since he'd closed his eyes. It actually looked like it was going to clear up. He was a country boy at heart and had spent most of his adult life in San Diego where it rarely rained. But rain didn't bother him. He was as at home in water as he was on land and in the sky.

Rinsing, he looked at the tent again, his affection filling up his chest. She was a tough cupcake, even with all those tantalizing sprinkles. She'd kept up with him and hadn't lost her cool, not once, even during those firefights. The determination on her face when she'd picked up that stick was mixed in with a healthy dose of fear. *Gators* were intimidating, but Dana had every intention of coming back into the water to help him. He smiled broadly at that, chuckled, and shook his head.

Clicking sounds came from the tent. "Are you laughing because I'm the worse guard you've ever seen?"

He turned to find her on her knees, tucking her phone behind her, peeking out of the tent flaps. She looked so delectable, sleep-flushed and drowsy. He crouched down. "No, I was thinking about you armed with that stick and all that courage against a "creepy" reptile with very pointed teeth that probably outweighed you."

"Hey, I could have taken him, her, it." She giggled.

It was impossible not to kiss her. He went to his knees, grabbed her by the back of the neck and pressed his mouth over hers. She made a surprised sound, then her mouth softened against his, and she kissed him back, her hand clenched around his wrist.

"So I guess this means you forgive me for my obviously suspect lookout skills?

"Since we're still in one piece, yup. Let's get going before I push you inside that tent and start something that is going to slow us down considerably."

"Of course, pushing would be involved." She ran her thumb over the fullness of his bottom lip.

"Plenty of pushing," he growled. He kissed her again. "Hours of pushing." Their gazes collided, and her animated honey brown eyes were so warm and teasing. This woman who had captured his senses, his body, and his imagination was a lot like the fighter he was and just as adaptable.

"Hoo boy," she said, her voice breathless. "Yeah...what were we doing?"

He ran his hand through her silky hair, but a snap in the distance had him turning on a dime and facing outward, his pistol out of the holster, trained on whatever threat was out there. He blocked Dana with his body. She put her hands on his bare shoulders with a soft gasp.

A jaguar padded out of the trees, its mouth open to show his teeth and pink tongue. "Dana, don't move."

He felt her chin hit his shoulder. "Wow, this is only the second time I've seen one of those, and the first time it was in a zoo."

He sighted it with the muzzle as it moved across their periphery. The big cat stopped, and those gold eyes swung toward them.

"How beautiful."

"Yeah. If he wants to stay that way, he better keep moving."

Her hands tightened on his shoulders, and her warm breath caressed his skin.

"Stop distracting me, woman."

"Really? Let's see how good that SEAL focus is."

"Dana," he said in warning, his eyes still on the stationary cat.

She nuzzled her nose into his neck. "Mm-hmm. Nice." She kissed his skin, and he growled. The cat lifted his head and his ears pricked forward. "They say jaguars are territorial." She breathed the words right into his ear, and he gritted his teeth, blowing air out of his mouth in one continuous stream.

When she licked him, his intake of breath made her smile against his skin. He made a soft sound in his throat when she bit him. His whole body jerked, going on red hot alert, but he kept his eyes on the animal.

"I wonder if it would be beneficial to have this kind of training in BUD/S. You know, have some women sign up to kiss hot male necks while they're supposed to be focusing on, you know, battle stuff."

"Dammit, Dana."

"Maybe I should flash my tits and ass at you. You could call that T & A training." She kissed and licked him again. "And speaking of asses. Yours is...spectacular. I know because I've been following it through all of this jungle for days."

He growled and the cat continued to watch them.

"I have to admit, I want to see you buck ass naked, Bowie," she whispered, her breath driving him crazy, his name on her lips turning him on even more. "Not a stitch on all that beautiful, muscled skin. I need about an hour to trace every inch with my tongue. Can you schedule that in somewhere?"

He was aching now, willing the freaking predator to move off so he could throttle that damn sexy woman.

"I bet this is the first time you got a hard-on while completely focused on imminent danger." His chest heaved as he panted heavily. "Let's see if my calculations of hot breath, neck kissing...ah...carry the licking and add in talking dirty equation equals a huge, gorgeous boner." She pressed her breasts to his back. "Tell me, handsome. Did I do the math right?"

When he felt her hand slide over his throbbing dick, his muffled groan made her laugh softly. "Oh, yeah, I'm so good at math," she whispered. "I think I deserve an A, don't you?" She squeezed his ass, then rubbed him through his pants. "I'd settle for a huge, hard B."

Finally, blessedly, the cat got bored and slunk off to his right. As she fondled him, her hand going to his chest as she ran her hands over his biceps in a slow, aching caress, manhandling his pecs, slipping down to his abs, he didn't take his eyes off the animal.

As soon as he disappeared from sight, Ruckus spun, taking her down into a tackle, flat on her back in the tent. She let out a peal of laughter and he joined her. He couldn't remember ever feeling this light in his life.

"You're..."

"Cute, sexy, amazing, beautiful."

"A fucking pain in the ass."

"Would that be this ass?" He currently had his dick right up against the heat of her, and she wrapped her legs around him, her hand cupping both cheeks and tightening.

"Son of a bitch."

She held his eyes with a sultry, disarming gaze. Before

she could utter another sexy word, he captured her mouth
with his. Her lips parted as she sucked in a quick, startled
breath. He shoved his fingers into her hair and held her
head in his hands, keeping her immobile as he delivered a
demanding, open-mouthed, tongue-tangling kiss he knew
she wanted.

8

Above her, his body responded to the warmth and softness of her supple curves, hardening him in a scalding rush of need. He was being reckless, his duty taking a back seat to his needs that had been denied so long.

She had pushed him into this with her cute as hell dirty talking. His mouth descended on hers like a starved man's. And that's exactly how he felt...ravenous, greedy, demanding.

Her heady scent seemed to be everywhere and infused every breath he managed to inhale. With her breasts warm and yielding against his chest, he had the overwhelming urge to touch her everywhere at once to drown each of his five senses with her essence and sensuality.

Keeping his mouth on her, he went to his knees, sliding his hands down. He undid her pants. Grasping both hands around the waistband, he pulled them down and off her. He popped his button and unzipped enough to get his dick out, pulling her closer and fitting the hard ridge of his erection between her thighs. The soft, needy sound she made in the back of her throat, combined with the provocative way she rolled her hips against his, had his blood roaring in his ears and pure need surging through his body.

That easily, she'd pushed him to this madness. And now that he'd let go, he'd lost the ability to slow down or stop. He couldn't stop, even if his life depended on it. And at the moment, his life depended on kissing her, touching her, and feeling her hot and wet around him.

"Bowie," she whispered his name into his ear, her breath sending tingles all along his nerve endings. He pushed into her, then deeper, filling her, and her inner muscles clamped tightly around him. Her head rolled, and she panted for air. His body shuddered, and he buried his face against her neck, his ragged breath blowing over her heated skin.

"So tight, so hot and wet," he rasped. He reached between them, caressing her, stroking her rhythmically for several minutes, the pressure building and building. She let out a cry and arched sinuously against him. Without giving her a chance to fully recover from her orgasm, he grasped both her wrists, pulled her arms up, and pinned them above her head, giving him complete control of the situation.

He settled more fully on top of her, his thighs forcing hers farther apart, and then he pressed his dick into her over and over again, setting his body on fire. He crushed his mouth to hers and kissed her deeply, the taste of her something he wouldn't ever get enough of. He was lost in her.

He plunged into her, fast and deep and strong, a rich, seductive rhythm that pulsed as vitally as his heartbeat. His hips ground against hers with each thrust until he felt her go rigid against him and he let go. A low growl erupted from his chest and vibrated through them. With a violent jerk, his lower body arched into her high and hard, riding those aching, flexing pulses until he came in a blinding climax of intoxicating speed and throbbing sensation.

Unable to get enough of her soft body, he rested against her. His lungs felt tight, his breathing labored as though he'd been running for miles. Blood pounded in his temples, and his heart thundered against the wall of his chest. He should never have touched her. Now, what was he going to do? She was under his skin...had been working her way there over the course of this cluster of an op. Dana had the kind of presence that couldn't be ignored—the scent of her, the softness of her skin beneath his hands, the taste of her on his tongue—and the gripping need to drive inside her and make her his was too potent to overcome. At that moment, nothing else mattered.

Never had a woman affected him on such a primitive, I-need-to-get-you-now level, but Dana had had that effect on him since day one. She had him at baby blue terry cloth. It had just been a matter of time before they acted on their mutual attraction. Their confrontations and arguments had just been freaking foreplay.

"Are we ever going to get naked?"

"Not today, cupcake. Not out here."

She nodded, a sated, sexy smile curving her lips. It was all he could do not to do her all over again. "So it's a battle fuck then?"

His laughter erupted at her words. Her eyes were full of mischief and so alive. She looked...beautiful, and he couldn't help but touch her again, caress her soft, warm cheek with the back of his knuckles and smooth her disheveled hair away from her face. The depth of tenderness weaving through his system startled him, and he dismissed the thoughts filtering through his mind before he followed through on them.

He'd been bitter for so many years. Maybe it was just too late for him to ever recover and have anything that was real and true in his life. Or maybe he was too damn stubborn. Whatever it was, he knew this was temporary. Overcome by adrenaline and pure, unadulterated mutual attraction.

"Battle fuck?"

"Yeah, a quick one between conflict."

"I'm sorry..." he began.

Her eyes sparkling, she breathed, "Oh, no. You have nothing to be sorry for, at all. That was...delicious."

Something unknotted inside his chest, and he smiled. "You are a warrior."

"I think that might be the nicest thing you've ever said to me."

He moved off her and they cleaned up. He had to admit, he had driven her hard, partly to keep her off balance and partly to keep his mind off doing her up against the nearest tree.

After they had eaten, packed up the tent, and shouldered their packs, she said in a soft voice, "You should laugh more often. You have a nice one."

"And ruin all this aggressive male shit I have going here? Not on your life. Now get that shapely ass in motion, babe."

Before he could lead the way, she grabbed his shoulder and said, her voice low and sweet, "That was the best sex I've ever had in my life."

He tipped up her chin. "Really? Well, wait until I get you somewhere we can safely get naked. We'll have battalion sex."

"Battalion sex. Oh, my. I don't think I can wait. Is that a big, never-ending column of power?"

He chuckled. "God help me. You do have a way with words," he said as he stepped toward the trees.

Pointing to herself, she laughed and said, "Reporter."

They trekked for miles, the jungle so thick in places,

razor-sharp thorns would have torn them apart if he didn't have the machete, a requirement in this overgrown monstrosity of an ecosystem.

He was soaked through again, but the culprit wasn't the rain. It was the moisture-rich jungle and his own sweat.

"This looks familiar," Dana said, then he stopped, and she plowed into him. There was a skull on a stake, a warning to people that the FARC owned this territory. The surface was rain-polished to a shine, the jawbone missing. It seemed symbolic of the fact that the dead couldn't talk. "Not far from here is *Palo de Letras*, Panama's border. There's a stone obelisk marking the divide." Moving on, they came out to a worn trail. "This is it," she whispered, her voice hushed in the dusk. In the deepening gloom, he saw a poured-concrete marker, part of the *Carretera del Darién*, a through-highway that was never built. There was a hubcap from a Chevrolet Corvair, casualty of a 1961 expedition. Ruckus looked up as the *whop, whop* of rotor blades from one of the Senafront helicopters beat in the sky.

"Rogue One to Ruckus, over."

He touched his throat mic. "Ruckus, over."

"Boss," Scarecrow said. "We've been out of touch both by satellite and by radio because of the storms. We're about ten miles out. Do you have a location for Salazar?"

"Negative. Give me five." He keyed the mic off.

He turned to her and grasped her arms. "Dana, where is Salazar?"

She bit her lip and looked away. "You promise you'll let me go with you."

He wasn't big on lying, but Dana was adamant that she was going with him, and he couldn't let her. Salazar was dangerous, and he wanted her back. He wasn't going to give the bastard the opportunity to snatch her up again. "I promise. Now tell me. We're going to find the nearest village after that and get something to eat, regroup and resupply. Then it's Salazar."

She searched his eyes, and he guessed she was happy with what she saw. He immediately felt guilty but pushed it aside. He had his orders. Get the woman to safety and get the package by any means.

"He's in Santa Clara at the resort there. He's mixing business with pleasure, some woman he met in Panama City. Something urgent came up with his Mexican partners. He's going to be there for another week, I think."

"A working vacation? Just outside of Panama City?"

"Yes. I guess even drug runners and murderers need a break."

He shook his head. This was a bit more complicated. Bagging Salazar at a busy resort was going to take some finesse, some recon, and a whole hell of a lot of planning. But first he had to get Dana out of harm's way and on a plane back to the States, find transpo, and get himself some civvies nice enough for a resort. The problem was he had no cash on him.

He keyed his mic and relayed the information to his team.

"What are your orders, sir?"

"Get some cash somehow—"

"I have cash," Dana interrupted.

"Standby," Ruckus said. He turned his head slowly and met her gaze. "You have cash? Why?"

She gave him a wry smile. "For porters, equipment, bribes, and stuff."

He frowned. This woman never ceased to amaze him. "How much do you have?"

"Seven thousand," she said as if she was going to loan him twenty bucks.

"What? On you?"

She gave him a patient look. "I have a concealed pouch in my pack, so yes, on me. Most of it is American, but I have some of it in pesos."

"Son of a bitch. That will do." He said into the mic, "Belay the order for cash."

Dana moved off, searching the skies.

"Instead, go to the airport and scope it out. We need to get her on the next possible flight."

"The cupcake package?" Wicked asked, amusement in his voice.

"Yeah, the cupcake package. Make sure it's all clear before I bring her in."

"Copy that, LT. Rogue One out."

A burst of gunfire in the distance propelled Ruckus into motion. He ran up the trail and grabbed her arm and dragged her off into the trees. Before he realized it, they were surrounded by so many armed men, they couldn't move. He whispered, "Stay here. I'm going to make a hole and we're going through it."

Before she could protest, he was grabbing the only claymore he had, a detonable bomb filled with metal balls that would disperse into the kill zone like a shotgun blast. But he had to get close enough to punch the hole for them to get through.

With automatic weapons fire and explosions going off all around him, he sprinted into the melee and deposited the mine behind a log. Then he ran full out back toward Dana's position. Her wide, terrified eyes showed nothing but relief when he returned. He grabbed her head and pressed it against his chest, shielding her the best he could with his body. He blew the mine, and the sound of it was deafening, drowning out everything. Before the sound waves of the blast had fully spread, he was up and running with Dana in tow. They slipped through the hole he'd made, avoiding the bodies littering the ground.

Once through, he kept going. The confusion of the blast along with the armed conflict hid them effectively from notice.

It was dark when they made the small town, a community of round, thatch-roofed huts that sloped up the mountainside to slash-and-burn plots. Going around to the back of one of the homes, he pulled some clothes off a makeshift line: two pairs of khaki pants, a light blue T-shirt, a blue cotton shirt, and a couple pairs of boxer briefs. In the dense overgrowth, just beyond the small hut, he changed, stuffing his uniform and spare clothes into the pack. He broke down his M4, stowing the pieces inside as well, but buckled his sidearm back on, covering it with the loose shirttail.

He shouldered his pack and took her hand. "Let me do the talking," he said. "I speak fluent Spanish."

"I do, too," she said in Spanish. She accessed her secret pouch and pulled out a substantial amount in pesos, giving the money to him.

"Nice, but let's keep this simple. We get food, a room, hopefully with a shower, and a good night's rest in a bed. Then we restock and buy a boat. We can take the river the rest of the way to Yaviza, then grab transpo once we get there to take us into Panama City."

She nodded. "Agreed. A bed sounds wonderful."

That phrase conjured up so many sensual thoughts, he had to work to keep his mind on the here and now. He took her hand again and went onto the main thoroughfare and soon came to a cantina. Holding her hand as if they were a couple felt realer than he wanted to feel. His protective instincts, her strength in the face of threat and danger and the reminder that he'd been lonely for a long time mixed him up inside. Made him think about how it would be to really be with her...as a couple. There were a number of people occupying the tables, chairs and the barstools. He walked up to the bar, people giving them curious looks. "Hi. We're looking for food and a place to stay. You have anything available?"

The woman smiled and nodded, introducing herself as Sienna, giving him a price for a room. She was British, her accent thick. "That include a shower?" She nodded again. He paid her, and then they got a meal of fried fish and rice. It tasted a lot better than the MREs.

EVER SINCE HE'D run into all those flying bullets, Dana had this horrible feeling in her stomach, and the food, although quite tasty, did nothing to alleviate it. She couldn't get the image out of her head. She still felt shell-shocked and, damn it, close to tears.

Needing some distance from him, she pushed back her chair and rose. He glanced up with a quizzical look, and she said, "I'm going to talk to Sienna about some clothes."

He nodded and returned to his scrutiny of the bar and the surrounding area.

"Hi," she said approaching the bar. "I'm pretty much out of clean clothes and I was hoping to maybe buy something off you. Could you spare anything?" Dana was more than just attracted to Ruckus, she was harboring feelings for him. Tentative feelings because she was well aware that their situation was temporary. What had happened between them had been random, but it hit home that her relationship with Jeffrey was weak and her feelings for him, albeit friendly, weren't of the romantic kind. She'd deluded herself because it had been so comfortable with him.

"Of course. Please follow me." Sienna went through a doorway behind the bar into a small apartment. There was a kitchen off to the right next to a closed door. She ducked into an adjacent room, motioning for Dana to follow her. Despite the heat and the humidity, it wasn't bad inside. Sparse, but neat and tidy, just like the bar.

Inside the small room, she went to a set of drawers and opened one, pulling out a couple pairs of pants, then two shirts. "Will these do?"

They were clean and dry. After what Dana's current clothes had been through, they were heavenly. "Oh, God, yes. Thank you. How much?"

"Give me your dirty clothes, and I'll get them cleaned for you for a small price. Is that fair?"

"Yes, totally. I'll bring them to you later."

A weak, old voice called out, and Sienna looked toward the doorway. "Oh, excuse me. Why don't you try them on to see if they fit? I'll be right back."

Dana didn't want to get them that close to her, so she held them up and decided they would be fine. After a few minutes, Sienna came back. "I'm sorry. That's my mother. She's ill."

Her heart tightened, reminding her so much of her mom and her struggles with her own illness. "No apologies necessary. I'll let you get back to work. Thanks again."

She came back out into the cantina. Since Ruckus had already gotten the key, he was waiting for her. They headed out the door to the adjoining structure. Entering, they went to the numbered room and unlocked the door. Pushing it open, Dana sighed with appreciation. A bed. A real honest-to-God bed. It wasn't much, but it was a damn sight better than a tent on the lumpy ground in the middle of the jungle hands down. Feeling shaky, she said, "You can shower first." Shucking off her pants, she then sank down onto the bed. "I'm going to enjoy this luxury for a minute." Thinking about being with him again got her juices flowing. Ruckus had layers and layers. She now knew he was a complicated man, a worthy man, one she could sink into and work on discovering even more about him. Getting physical with him had been amazing, but she realized this was an isolated situation. They had been thrown together and had to rely on each other to get through to where they were now. He had been hurt in his past and that had made him draw into himself. She could understand that, but she had to keep all this in perspective. When the mission was over, they would go their separate ways. Him back to the SEALs and his life in San Diego and her back to her own life where she had some hard thinking to do.

But what she needed was some processing time to work through all the stuff that had happened since she'd decided to make this trip into the Darién.

WHEN HE CAME out of the ramshackle shower, she was still sitting cross-legged on the bed. It was as if she hadn't moved since they came into the small room. The towel around his waist hid his rigid dick. The adrenaline in his system was riding him hard, resulting in a hard-on aching and painful with need. He couldn't reconcile his soft feelings for her with his lifestyle and his job. This unexpected situation with her was more than a cluster, it was feeling like a life-changing situation. But he was so bad at relationships. He wasn't sure he could let go of his past bitterness and mistrust. He towel-dried his hair, the thin material obscuring his vision for a moment. Trying to keep it light, he said with a chuckle, "That shower isn't big enough for a mouse." When he dropped the towel, he saw her face and rushed across the room. "Babe, what is it?"

She was crying. Through this whole ordeal, he hadn't seen her shed a tear— a woman's most potent secret weapon—but now they were tracking down her face. He swallowed hard. He knew how to insert into enemy territory right under the enemy's nose, blow shit up, and kill a man with his bare hands. But this...this was delicate, and he wasn't a delicate man. He was a hard badass, but Dana had gotten under his armor, and he couldn't figure out how to get her out.

When she didn't say anything, he didn't know what to do. He panicked, wrapped his arms around her, and drew her hard against him, rocking her gently. "Tell me how to make it right?"

She pressed her hot face against his damp skin, her tears mingling with the moisture already there. He cupped the back of her head and said, "C'mon, babe, I'm flying blind here."

"I had no idea," she whispered. "No idea." She gasped on a shuddering sigh.

"About what?" He leaned back so he could see her beautiful face. Framing it, he said gently, "You're safe with me."

She shook her head. "Maybe physically...no, maybe not even that. But I had no idea until just now."

He stiffened. "What the fuck do you mean? I wouldn't hurt you. I say I'm going to throttle you, but that's just mean

SEAL man talk when you get me so mad I want to chew nails."

With a half-hearted chuckle, she said, "You're so clueless. I feel safe with you, but it feels dangerous at the same time."

"Dangerous? Because I'm a SEAL." He was struggling here. He was used to conversing with men who said what the hell they meant, not some riddling woman who was making a freaking crossword puzzle out of a simple conversation.

"Oh, God. Protect me from dense men. Do I really need to spell it out?"

Ruckus tried to be patient, but he wasn't a patient man. Action was really his middle name. "Babe...so help me, spill before I go insane."

"You're the kind of guy that runs toward the bullets and not away from them."

For a minute, he just didn't get it. What was she talking about? Of course he ran toward conflict. He was a SEAL. It took him a moment to tamp down his confusion. "Ah, do I need to give you my resume? It's what I do. It's my job, and out there is my office."

With a slight smile and an intense look, she said, "But when you have a bad day at the office, you have a really bad day."

He laughed and dragged her against him. "That's true. But it comes with the territory, just as your smart, sassy mouth comes with your territory."

Her eyes narrowed and was it crazy? He just loved her like this, giving back just as good as he gave. Dealing with her complicated feelings for him wasn't something he wanted to face. Her sass let him off the hook for his own vulnerability. Things were getting much too real with this woman. "Don't start. I'm trying to have a moment here," she growled.

"What kind of moment and could you make it fast? You smell and need a shower."

She rolled her eyes and wiped at her tears. "You are *such* a gentleman."

"Aw, no. Not me. No GQ here, just Ruckus."

"Yeah, that's what's driving me insane."

"You, too?"

She smiled a long-suffering smile, shoved him hard, and got off the bed, heading toward the shower. Before she went through the door, she turned to him. "I'm only going to say this to you because you saved my life, and I'm having a momentary lapse in judgment where you're concerned."

He reclined, his body surging every moment. For them, this was foreplay. "Lay it on me."

"You're brave. I've never seen courage before. Oh, yeah, maybe the silent kind when my mom was dying from cancer, but not straight out, take-no-prisoners, full-metal jacket, freaking pull-out-all-the-stops bravery. I'm blown away, you idiot. I care for you. I care what happens to you."

"Does that mean I can get some?" he asked, deadpan. She whipped off her shirt and threw it at him with an exasperated, huffing laugh. "You are such a bastard."

He caught it, the material still warm from her body. "That's a yes." He smirked and slipped off the bed, stalking toward her. "Because, babe, adrenaline gives me a fucking hard-on like you wouldn't believe. Like making love all night kinda erection."

"You just said that the shower isn't big enough for even a mouse."

"Did I say that? Fuck, it's not even big enough for my damn dick. He reached her, and his body went even more rigid if that was possible. Adrenaline and Dana equaled the biggest, baddest, I've-got-to-be-inside-her-for-hours erection. He dragged her up against him, and she let out a soft moan when she felt that bad boy between her legs. "Oh, that's a definite yes. So, I'm a SEAL, I'll improvise."

"You won't need to. I'm not letting you touch me until I'm as clean as you are."

"What?"

She pressed her hand in the middle of his chest and shoved him a step out the door, then shut it in his face.

"Well, hell," he muttered.

9

Another small modern convenience that she had taken for granted. A simple shower. She took her time, still working at the emotion that was tying her up in knots. As long as she lived, she would never forget the sight of him running toward such danger. She didn't want to cry in front of him again. With trembling fingers, her body still on fire, she rubbed vigorously at her hair, no blow dryer in sight, so she combed and braided it to keep the wet strands out of her way.

Tucking the end of the towel right between her breasts, she opened the bathroom door and stopped dead. She was met with the most arousing sight she'd ever seen in her life.

Bowie was on the bed, naked except for his dog tags. His thick erection hadn't abated, because his hand was wrapped around it. His eyes were closed and his face taut with pleasure.

Her stomach did a free-fall tumble that had nothing to do with the emotions she had been wrestling with and everything to do with her intense attraction to Bowie. God, the man was so sinfully gorgeous he ought to be deemed illegal. Especially the way he was working his shaft, exuding an earthy, sexual magnetism, one she was finding dangerous on so many levels—physically, emotionally, mentally, just as she'd told him. The fact that this man had the ability to affect her so completely was a scary prospect she wasn't prepared to deal with.

She wanted to remember him like this when they did part ways.

"Are you starting without me?"

He chuckled, a low, rumbling sound that stimulated her from head to toe. He stirred, his eyes opening slowly and only to half-mast over that heartbreaking, velvety blue. A dark brow lifted lazily, as did one corner of his mouth.

"Nope, just keeping things at attention."

He reached up, but she slapped his hand away. "Just give me a minute, Lieutenant Pushy. I'm still taking a tour of what you have to offer." It was a lot of gorgeousness to take in with his broad shoulders, wide, heavily muscled chest, rounded biceps, his erection lying on a set of very impressive abs, and a tantalizing line of hair leading to a woman's bliss.

"Are you? Seems to me that I should be accorded the same courtesy." She stood there, his hot blue eyes caressing every inch of her, the tension increasing with each passing second. "C'mon, cupcake, get rid of the towel. I'm dying to see you." Even when he was pleading, he was all arrogant, presumptuous male.

Unable to refuse him anything—or herself, for that matter—she set her hand at the tuck of the towel and released the tension. As the terry fell away, his eyes flashed, taking in the whole length of her, his face softening. "Damn, babe."

She put a knee on the bed, unable to take her eyes off all

his naked flesh and rippling muscles. She wanted to put her mouth so many places on his body, she was momentarily nonplussed. His dark hair was tousled and spiky, thick and glossy, adding to his badass appeal.

"I really like the way you're looking at me, but I'd like more action." When she didn't move, he grabbed her by the waist and lifted her on top of him. Her heart stuttered and then resumed its frantic pace. She dipped her head down, covering his tantalizing mouth, the stubble on his face scratchy and arousing. She kissed her way to his chin, breathing deep of his scent, a mixture of soap and sex. "Ride me, cupcake. I need that sugar rush."

It was an order she wasn't going to refuse. Aching to taste him, all of him, continuing the sensual journey, she moved down the column of that strong throat, licking the taut cords. Then to the hard points of his rigid nipples. She laved them, grazed the tips with the edge of her teeth, her nails scraping over his rib cage down to his waist. A groan rumbled from his chest as she traveled her way lower, spreading hot, wet kisses on his rippled abs. Then she used the tip of her tongue and her nails on the tantalizing flesh just above his erection while he sucked in a surprised breath in response to her ministrations. She bit his hip and he jerked, his breath ragged.

She wrapped her fingers around the hard, velvet-textured length of him and felt him pulse in her tight grip. A drop of fluid appeared, and she rubbed the silky moisture over the plum-shaped head of his cock.

She took him into her mouth, his skin hot and salty against the stroke of her tongue. He shuddered and wrapped her braid in his hand, and she sucked him, taking him as deep as she could, finally giving in to that fantasy she had out in the jungle. She pleasured him with her mouth, teased him with her tongue, and aroused him to a fever pitch of need that made his entire body shake with the restraint of trying to hold back.

"Oh, damn," he breathed and frantically tried to tug her back up. "If you don't stop doing that, I'm going to come."

Since she still had more interesting things she wanted to explore before he came, she complied. With one last irresistible lick along his shaft and a gentle suck at the tip that made him shift his hips and groan deep, she kissed her way back up his body until she was straddling him again, hard against his groin.

She guided his erection into her, so wet from where her mouth had been. Her sex stretched tight around his width as his nostrils flared, and stark desire burned in his eyes. He clutched her waist and rocked her tighter against his straining body, setting a rhythm she knew would take him quickly to orgasm.

She rolled her hips, and his head arched back, his face contorting with pleasure, his breathing fast. He groaned again, and his lost and mindless look only fueled her movements until she was rocking hard and fast on him.

"Dana," he whispered, jackknifing against her. His groan of surrender in her ear was the sexiest sound she'd ever heard.

For several heartbeats, he held her hard against him, his hand smoothing rhythmically up and down her back, both of them spent from running for four days. His body was hard beneath hers, so solid and warm.

When she lifted her head, she met his soft blue eyes, the desire banked. She pressed her mouth against his in a fierce kiss, then he shifted and rolled to his side, cradling her in his arms.

She was still working on coming down from the storm of

emotion, but she could at last collect her senses. She hugged him and stroked his hair, profoundly moved by the care he had taken with her since she'd met him, knowing the pleasure she had given him. Closing her eyes against the sting of tears and constriction in her throat, she continued to stroke his head, needing to give him comfort, so full of feeling for him that she could barely stand it. He had gone from this controlling jerk of a stranger to this guy who she knew better. But damn if she didn't want to know what fueled that anger she'd glimpsed more than once.

She ached for him to confide in her, but she couldn't expect him to go that far if he wasn't feeling it. Bowie tightened his hold on her, his chest expanding as he took a deep, unsteady breath. Fingering the soft silk of his hair, she kissed his temple, a nearly unbearable tenderness filling her chest.

"Damn, woman, I think you unraveled me."

"Then we're even," she whispered against his cheek.

Bracing his weight on one arm, he lifted his head, his touch leaving her breathless as he kissed her mouth, brushing his lips over hers, the caress gentle and searching. Inhaling unevenly, Bowie slid his arms around her in a warm, hard embrace, deepening the kiss as she smoothed her hand up the center of his back.

It was as though he couldn't get enough of that soft, caressing intimacy, and it was a long time later when he reluctantly eased away. Brushing strands of hair back with his knuckles, he lifted her chin and gave her another light kiss, then released his breath. "Sleep with me, beautiful," he whispered gruffly.

She melted more than she had since she'd met this man. She wrapped her arms around his neck and kissed him some more. She didn't know why, but the huskiness in his request made her want to cry. Fighting against the surge of emotion, and praying she wasn't making a mistake here, they crawled under the covers, both of them exhausted. She snuggled right up against all that muscle.

Sliding his hand up the back of her head, he deepened the kiss, molding her against him with the weight of his body. "I want to hold you, cupcake."

Overwhelmed by emotion, Dana enjoyed his embrace, her naked breasts hard against his chest. He captured one and kneaded it. Then he slipped his hand to her hip and across her back, separating her legs and settling her between his thighs. Dana's breath caught at the feel of his naked body molded fully against hers. Cupping her jaw, he kissed her, then nestled her head into the curve of his shoulder. "Go to sleep, babe," he whispered gruffly.

The room was still dark, but early-morning sounds were filtering in when Dana awoke. Hovering between awake, but not awake, she heard the water running and her eyes popped open. The small room, the small town...Ruckus... Bowie. Making love with him had, of course, changed things from their confrontational relationship to this new one. She was sure nothing about him had changed except for the way he looked at her now. He'd still be a hard-ass, pushy, it's the mission, ma'am, SEAL. No doubts. Expecting or thinking about a future with him would be counterproductive. After this trip, she was off to South Africa for a story on child soldiers, then traveling to a small city in Russia that was rumored to be a stop-off point for white slavery.

Her happiness wasn't important; there were so many people suffering in the world. If she could do one small thing to shine a light where there was darkness, she would.

With a hard shot to her gut, she remembered she did have to make a quick trip to San Diego and Jeff. There was no way she could continue a relationship with him now. She already knew it before she'd left for the Gap. She'd been a coward, trying to put off the inevitable because Jeff had been a port in the storm when her mom had died. He'd been so wonderful. She felt terrible, but nothing could overcome how she felt right now about the man who was only now in the bathroom.

She rose, closing her eyes, drawing up her knees and pulling the sheet around her, memories swarming in and making her go weak inside. She locked her arms around her legs and rested her forehead on her upraised knees, the flurry in her chest leaving her light-headed. Damn, but it had been unbelievable. But what made her pulse labor was recalling how she had wakened in the middle of the night and found Bowie curled around her back, his arms securing her against him, holding her in the shelter of his body.

The door opened, and Bowie materialized in the door frame. Damn, it was hard to take this man clothed, but naked—she felt as if the bed had just opened up beneath her and she was falling.

"Hey, cupcake. You look good enough to eat in the morning." He was obviously as unselfconscious of his body as he was everything else. Truly a man who led a SEAL team, confident in his orders and the split-second decisions he made on a daily basis.

He said "cupcake" with an inflection of affection now instead of that annoyed, impatient way he'd said it when they first met. Gaining this man's admiration was no small feat, and she felt totally jazzed that he had come to respect her.

"You're not bad yourself. I'm not sure if you realize this, but you're quite a hunk. Any woman would be happy to wake up to you."

Something dark and dangerous flashed behind his eyes before it disappeared. "I'm not interested in making any other woman happy right now," he said, walking to the bed. "You are it."

"Think you can expand on what went on here last night?"

"Ah, babe, I got that covered, tied down, locked up, tagged and bagged."

He tumbled her onto her back, and before her peal of laughter could subside, he had the sheet off her. He pushed her legs apart, moved in between them, slowly stroked his warm, callused palms up her thighs, until his thumbs caressed her intimately.

"You are amazing."

He grinned, and she was trembling in anticipation, and the rogue knew it, too. "I'm always about lifting the bar, sweetheart," he quipped huskily, and she caught the hot blue of his eyes as he settled his provocative body more comfortably against her. He nuzzled her thigh and applied a wet suction to a patch of flesh that made her gasp and would no doubt leave a mark.

The only problem: she already felt thoroughly branded by this man's heat, his touch, everything about him.

"If you keep looking at me like that, I'm going to lose my focus," he murmured.

"Too bad. I'll look at you any way I please."

He chuckled, his tongue swirling a path to where she ached for his attention the most, and she lost herself in him.

~

BY MID-MORNING THE NEXT DAY, she was feeling rested after two good nights of sleep in Bowie's arms. She had dumped out all the contents of both of their packs, assessed what they had—geez, the navy made sure their SEALs were well stocked in the field—and knew what they needed. Food was an issue, but if they got the boat Bowie was currently negotiating, it would be a quick ten-mile trip to Yaviza.

His throat mic was on the side table, and she was fascinated with it. She put in the earpiece and set the transponders against her own throat. It was more comfortable than she thought it would be.

"LT, airport is clear as a bell. Operation Cupcake is a go. We're ready to rendezvous with you at your orders."

Experiencing a sharp, hard twist to her heart, she quickly removed the apparatus without a response. She closed her eyes, trying to absorb the information that he had lied to her. He'd promised he'd take her with him, but it was clear he sent his men to the airport to make sure they could get her out without incident.

He'd "handled" her so that he could complete the mission. Dana closed her eyes and rubbed her forehead, a chill of comprehension making her insides shrink. She felt like a bomb ready to explode. Every sound sent her heart into overdrive. She finished packing the stuff back in the packs, then picked up the clothes she'd borrowed from Sienna.

Making her way to the cantina, she saw that Sienna wasn't there. She knocked at the doorway in the back that connected their small apartment to the bar, but there was no answer. Deciding to leave the clothes, she entered and set them on a small table just inside the open door and turned away. Before she took the steps out of their apartment, a weakened, muffled voice called out, urgency in her tone.

She turned to the closed bedroom door and looked toward the door leading out of the bar. The woman's frantic pleading got worse. Making a snap decision, she opened the door to find a lean, frail woman with iron gray hair lying loose on her pillow. Her moist eyes turned toward Dana, and she said plaintively, "So thirsty."

Dana hurried to the side table and poured water from a pitcher there, then sat down on the edge of the bed and supported the older woman so she could take a sip, then more. Her grateful, warm eyes thanked Dana as she drank her fill.

"That better?" Dana asked, the memory of her mom lying in her hospital bed, looking just as fragile, but the power of her gaze still as strong as ever, as fresh in her mind as if it had been yesterday. Pain and a deep sense of loss threatened to engulf her. That hollowness had been with her since the moment her father had called and delivered the devastating news. Her mom had died, alone and unexpectedly from a heart attack; the chemo, cancer, and stress to her body had been just too much.

There was no way Dana could have known, no way she could have gotten there in time. But other than the Darién Gap story, her mom had asked Dana to come home and spend her last moments being together as a family.

"Thank you, poppet," the woman said. "Bless you." Then she drifted back to sleep. It was hard to take the woman's gratitude, the guilt at failing her mom pressing hard against her heart.

A noise broke her concentration, and she looked up to see Bowie in the doorway. His face showed his compassion, aware of what she was struggling with. But her anger at his betrayal made her push everything away. She rose abruptly and brushed past him. Out in the cantina, she spied Sienna.

"I'm sorry. I didn't mean to intrude, but I was replacing

your clothes and your mother called out. I gave her some water. How ill is she?"

"Terribly. She was a missionary who came here to help. Then she got cancer and refused to go back home. I came out here and opened this place and have been nursing her, but with each day she fails. It won't be long until her suffering is over." Sienna's breath caught, and she covered her mouth. "It's been very hard."

Dana reached out and hugged her in a tight embrace, her eyes closing. "I know. My mom died from cancer. I wasn't there when it happened. I'm glad you're able to be here for your mom."

Her stricken eyes captured Dana's, the sympathy clutching at Dana's heart.

"I'm so sorry about your mom."

"Thank you," she whispered. She let go of Sienna and gave her one final bolstering look, then headed for her room. Bowie came in a few moments later. "Are you all right?"

"I'm fine."

"So that's a no."

She whirled on him. "You never had any intention of honoring my wishes, so you don't get to have a say in how I'm feeling now."

"What do you mean?"

"I know you're not taking me to Salazar."

He glanced at the bedside table and the throat mic. His features went taut. "Son of a bitch, Dana. It's too goddamned dangerous. You don't belong on a special op."

"Maybe not, but it's my choice to do this, and you're not taking that away from me. I'm an American citizen, and you can't force me to do anything."

He ran his hand through his hair. She dug in her pack,

adamant about what she had to do. She grabbed five hundred dollars and headed for the door.

He snagged her arm as she passed. "I have my orders. You're getting on that plane."

"I'm sure you do, but I have my own orders. You can go to hell."

She jerked her arm out of his grasp and slammed the door on her way out. Back in the bar, she approached Sienna and slipped the money into her hands. "Here, take this. Maybe it can help to get you something to ease your mom's pain."

Sienna looked down at the money and then up at her. "I couldn't—"

"Yes, you can," Dana said. "For her." Her eyes stung, her voice uneven. Tears filled Sienna's eyes and Dana's spilled over. She hugged Dana this time.

"God bless you." She tightened her hold. "*God bless you.*"

She was hoping that was true, because the moment she could, she was giving Ruckus the slip and going after Salazar herself. She would get those memory cards back. She had to, now more than ever.

10

Ruckus felt like a first-class jerk, but he couldn't get around his orders. Sometimes SEALs made split-second decisions in the field and went with their gut. His gut was saying that Dana was determined to do as she pleased. He had no reason to give in to a civilian and her foolhardy plans. Except he'd watched her give water to that old woman, the memories and the pain washing across her face. He'd read every regret, every sorrow. He *understood* why she wanted to go with him, and that all tore him up like nothing had in a long time.

He'd watched her with that old woman and knew she was remembering. She'd fought to school her breathing into a regular rhythm, blinked furiously at the moisture gathering in her eyes, busied herself with the welfare of the figure in the bed. Damn, she was a tough beauty. Once the lady had fallen asleep, there was no reason she shouldn't have just let go and bawled her eyes out if she wanted to. But she struggled to rein her emotions in, fought for control.

He sighed heavily.

She was getting on that plane. He just hated that she

would never forgive him. So, what the *hell*? He'd let another woman down. What else was new? At least she'd be alive and safe. So why did he feel so raw inside?

He'd negotiated for a boat, the small, wiry man jumping up and down until he got his desired price. Ruckus paid him, and he and Dana were leaving at nightfall for Yaviza. She had been giving him the cold shoulder ever since she'd heard through his mic that Wicked had secured the airport.

She was across from him shoveling in her food, focusing on it. He looked over to the bar where Sienna was taking care of customers. Dana had given the money she'd taken out of her pack to the young Brit.

It was a purely knee-jerk reaction on Dana's part, helping a young woman who was currently in the same boat Dana had been months ago, except, Ruckus got the feeling that she hadn't gotten closure.

This situation was volatile because there were deep emotions attached to those memory cards. Promises and guilt. A double-edged sword, sharp and dangerous—and poised between them. One of them would get cut. Ruckus had a feeling it'd be him. So he would have to take it a day at a time, living in each moment, breathing her in, absorbing every nuance. The heated fragrance of her bare skin beneath his palms, her lush, naked contours pressing to him and making him so hard he'd thought he'd come before he could even enter her. Dammit. The memory of her body jangled his nerves.

Ruckus felt like a man tottering on the brink of insanity and scowled. A little boy came into the bar and went to one of the stools. A man was slumped over there, and the boy tugged on the man's sleeve. He stirred and pushed the little boy away, but the kid, nerves of steel, went right back.

"Worthless little bastard..."

The voice came out of the past, out of his childhood. A voice beyond the grave. He flinched at the memory of that voice. A conditioned response, even after all this time. Often enough, a slurred line from his old man had been followed up with a back-hand across the mouth.

The image of his father rose up from one of the dark corners of his mind to taunt, and unable to help himself, he stood. Dana looked up at him, and something on his face must have alarmed her because she said, "Bowie?"

The memory of his mom sent anger shooting through him. The image of blood running from her nose and lip brought the rage he'd buried for so many years shooting into his gut like adrenaline. Tears swam in her eyes and streamed down her cheeks, but she didn't utter a word. His old man didn't like noise. Made him even meaner.

His eyes were riveted to the little boy now helping the man out of the bar. He followed them a few paces down the street. The man backhanded the kid, and he tumbled into a puddle. When he lunged at the kid, Ruckus was on him, shoving him against the wall, his fist landing in his father's face.

Just like he had all those years ago. When he'd been too small to help her, he'd tried anyway, and it had gotten him nothing but pain. But then he grew, matured, filled out, and the blow he'd delivered at seventeen knocked his father against the wall, out cold.

"Stop it, Bowie," Dana's voice pierced his memories, the fog lifting abruptly as the view of the bloodied stranger's face came into focus. He squeezed his eyes closed against it. He slammed his fist against the wall, the sounds of agony lost in the impact. He backed away from the man.

"Go home," he growled, and the drunk stumbled away. He turned to find the kid looking up at him, wet, shaking with the same look in his eyes that Bowie had seen in his own.

He knelt down and took the boy's small arms in his hands. "Don't ever let him make you feel worthless. You're not." He grabbed his chin. "Be strong."

The little boy's eyes flashed, and his chin lifted. He nodded curtly and then ran off down the street. For a moment, Bowie knelt there, breathing around his pain. Finally he felt her hands on him. "Come on," she whispered.

He rose, and they went back to their room, the meal forgotten. He went into the bathroom and turned on the water, hissing a little at the sting of the cuts on his knuckles, the blood, his own and the drunk's, washed down the drain.

He understood how she felt about her mother, but he had hated his father and hadn't mourned his passing for even a fraction of a second. The resentment was more acute that his mom had thrown him out. It hurt like a bitch, even now.

He wanted to let go of his bitterness and his pain, find some common ground and have a successful relationship out of the SEALs, but his role model had been so damaged, lost in a bottle, mean to the bone. Sometimes Bowie worried that he was just like him. If he didn't hate alcohol so much he might have even...he couldn't finish the thought.

When she came into the bathroom and took his hand, he tried to pull away, but she held on tight. She pressed her lips together and used the first aid kit to take care of his cuts.

When she was done, he left the room, brushing past her in the confines, the scent of her filling him up and pushing away the darkness.

He knew that old fears never quite died—they just hid in dark corners of the mind and waited for the chance to slip out.

He went to the window and looked out. "He deserved it," he said and believed every word. Maybe it would stop him from hitting the kid again, but Bowie didn't think so. There was nothing he could do for that kid, just like he'd been powerless with his own father.

"He did. Absolutely. But I don't care about him. How are you?"

He debated the wisdom of revealing anything about that time in his life. A part of him wanted to guard the secrets, hide the past, protect himself. "We should get a couple hours of sleep before we move out."

She came around in front of him. "Don't," she whispered and cupped his cheek. "He abused you, that's clear. Can you talk about it?"

He shrugged, as if it were unimportant or easy, when it was far from being either. "Yeah, old news."

"Apparently not."

Trying to hide anything from this woman who had shared the most private, intimate time with him, who had given him so much pleasure and held him safe in her arms, challenged him and surprised him, was pointless. She had opened her body to him; now he felt safe opening another part of himself, tentatively, hesitantly, feeling more vulnerable than he had in his life. "He was a mean, abusive drunk. I tried to fight back, but I was too small. Then I turned seventeen, and I clocked him, knocked him out cold. My mom threw me out after that."

"Did she? Maybe she wanted you to be safe. Maybe she wanted something better for you. Maybe she knew you were strong enough to survive, and she wanted to give you that chance before the violence closed off your freedom."

"Closed off my freedom?"

"Bowie, the violence could have gotten worse. I bet she knew that."

He'd never thought about that. He'd been mired in his bitterness. He'd never considered that his mom cared enough about him to make him go. She would have been trapped with him and his moods.

He thought about all the years that had passed. The years she had endured when he was alive, and now, Bowie had cut off any ties with her completely. He tried to breathe around that revelation, but his lungs couldn't seem to expand to accommodate the humid air. The pressure was so great, he wondered wildly if he would simply explode.

He needed control.

His hands balled into tight fists at his side as he tried to leash the fury building inside him. His whole body trembled with the power of it. If there wasn't rage and pain, there was now guilt.

"I wished him dead so many times, I lost count. He robbed us both," he whispered, his voice strained. He covered his eyes for a minute, trying to swallow past the emotion clogging his chest, rising in his throat.

"Oh, Bowie." She clasped him around the waist and pressed her face against his. "It's not too late." He watched her blink rapidly, as if she were afraid to take her eyes off him for even a fraction of a second. She held her ground, that was for sure, brave as all get out. And his heart squeezed painfully at the thought.

A fresh surge of hate for his father welled up inside him, and he recognized that a large part of his anger was from the fact that he had never been made to pay for his crimes. Justice had never been served. Some of the blame for that was his, he knew, and the guilt for that was terrible. If only he had found the courage to refuse to go or tell someone at school. But he hadn't.

His mother had been the one to suffer the price. Regret burned like acid in his throat, behind his eyes. He clenched his jaw against it, whipped himself mentally to get past it.

"Come on." She coaxed him toward the bed. "Let's get a couple hours of sleep before we have to go." He moved with her, relieved that she wasn't giving him the cold shoulder anymore. Somewhere along this journey with her, he found that he needed her. But that was something he would have to get over. He wasn't convinced that he could take any steps to make himself feel better. Not sure he could bridge the gap between his past and present, release the hatred and bitterness that had been so much a part of his life. It had fueled his anger, allowed him to excel as a SEAL. The team was his family.

But he took the comfort she offered as she smoothed her hands over him in the dark. He'd struggled with female relationships his whole life. After the horrible failure of his marriage, he had never let another woman get close, never this close. Abandonment was always there in his mind, lurking, and he left before they could leave him. It was his pattern. But Dana, she broke down his defenses with her understanding and her compassion. He admired her courage and her fortitude. She was like no one he'd ever met before.

Once his orders were given, he didn't deviate unless he reassessed everything and found the decision to not be sound. He was decisive. Lives depended on his leadership. Her life depended on it.

Dana was a complicated woman, and she'd shared only a brief glimpse of who she was. Outside she was strong and confident.

Inside she was lost. Like him.

Hours later, in the dark, they made their final preparations and walked through the town to the dock. They loaded up the boat, and the motor was the only sound that broke the hush of the forest.

The breeze was warm with a mixture of fertility, decay, and fish on the wind. As they passed pockets of green, the cacophony of the inhabitants of the forest made sure it was never really quiet out here.

He wrestled and struggled with the concept of letting a civilian accompany him on a top-secret black ops mission. It went against his orders to get her on that plane. Miles of trekking with her, protecting her, had changed their relationship ten-fold. He wasn't the same guy who had HALO'd into the jungle.

She had changed him.

His butt could be in a sling, his very career on the line, and that was his life, his family, and it terrified him to think about being out, disgraced. It made him sick, in fact.

His father had been a piss-mean, drunken, good-for-nothing son of a bitch who had told him time and again he would never be anything but a good-for-nothing son of a bitch. Bowie had proved him wrong, both about his lethal name and what he could accomplish.

But he had to admit, Dana wasn't just a civilian. Something had happened between them. When they had been locked together on that bed after her shower, his barriers had been obliterated. Her features had softened, her brown eyes glowed with more than open desire, and Ruckus didn't know what he wanted from her, if she gave a damn, but his body inside hers was more than two people satisfying a need.

Oh, yeah, it was something. And, fuck him, but he wanted more.

He couldn't dismiss what this meant to the cupcake, to *Dana*. It was closure for her, and she was willing to risk her life for it. That's what he couldn't seem to reconcile or ignore. If he was being honest with himself, his orders suited him just fine. He wanted to keep her safe, dammit. But the way she had looked at him, the fierceness in her eyes when she'd told him she was getting her memory cards back had been as fierce as any SEAL.

The soft sound of the motor echoed off the trees that crowded the shore, a no man's land beyond, one he'd traversed with this beautiful woman sitting quietly beside him. Voices travelled easily over the water, and he'd cautioned her about talking.

"What you did for Sienna," he whispered, keeping his voice low. "That was admirable."

"I didn't do it to garner your admiration," she said stiffly. The woman who had held him last night, comforted him, was gone. The lie he'd told her now sat between them.

"It's clear to me what's driving you, Dana."

"I'm so glad you get it, Bowie," she said, her eyes snapping and sarcasm dripping from her voice.

He was undeterred. His secrets were out in the open, and she'd actually helped him. He flexed his knuckles on the hand he'd slammed against the wall, close to that man's face he'd wanted to smash again. But the anger was that of a teenager. It was now time to take control of it, be a man and let go of the hatred he held for his father. It was the only way to move on. All this time, she'd been right. His father was controlling him, and now that he realized that, he wasn't going to let it get the best of him. Never again.

"Did your mother love you?"

She glared at him as if she wanted to smack him hard across the face. "Yes, she loved me."

"How do you know that?"

"Because...she told me. She showed me. She was always there for me, supporting me, taking care of me, giving me advice." Her eyes narrowed, the guilt and grief riding her hard. "After your failed marriage, you can be a good judge? Why did she leave you, Bowie?"

That hit him hard, making his own guilt tighten. "We're not talking about my failures here. We're talking about yours."

Her hands clenched into fists and she glared at him, angry tears filling her eyes. "You would be an expert, then."

"Yeah. Did you love her?"

"Yes," she snapped as if she couldn't quite understand where he was going with this questioning. "You know I still do."

"So, as she lay dying alone, was she really alone? Wasn't she thinking about you and your father. Even though time was short, I am sure she never thought less of you. That she would have gone into death still loving you."

Her face contorted, and she huddled into herself, her shoulders pulled in tight. The agony on her face, the gut-wrenching pain in her eyes hollowed him out; her tears shredded him. "She loved you, Dana. That's forever. It wouldn't have changed, and nothing you do or put yourself through will change it. So cut yourself some slack, and stop punishing yourself for not being there when she died. Sometimes promises are held in the heart even when they can't be redeemed. You don't have to suffer and sabotage your own happiness to atone for anything. I guarantee that it didn't matter that you weren't there in person. You were there in her heart, and her love for you carried her through."

She didn't say a word, only stayed turned away from him. Her soft crying he hoped washed away her guilt, freed her from the terrible pain, let her begin to mourn for her mom.

His throat tight, he looked away from her toward the banks thick with patches of yellow spiked cane and coffee weed, fan-fronded palmetto trees, and verdant ferns. The Gap was teeming with danger, but it also held a primitive beauty. Unable to handle it, he turned back and pulled her against him, wrapped his arm around her. She turned her hot, wet face into his neck, weeping in earnest as her tears soaked into his T-shirt, and his heart constricted against her sorrow.

Her sobs subsided, and there was nothing but sniffles as they passed through a shadowy corridor of trees. The sounds of branches rustling were most likely disturbed monkeys vaulting from one bough to the next. She still held onto him, and he assuaged his guilty conscience with the hope that his words had some impact on her, just as hers had an impact on him.

They made Yaviza as dawn was breaking across the jungle, the sky layered in orange, then a smoky white that lightened to a lush purple stain across the horizon, finally giving way to a bold, brilliant azure. She moved out of his embrace, her red-rimmed eyes the only sign that she'd gone through a deep emotional breakdown.

He spied the dock and activity as citizens of Yaviza prepared for the day on the water. Rivers were the highways of this region. He guided the boat over to the dock, settled between two boats and tied off the *piragua*. He went to help Dana up to the dock, but she was already moving. Transportation on his mind, he maneuvered to the dock and followed her. The town was bustling for so early in the morning, but she seemed to know where she was going. They would bus out, get to Panama City, then to the airport where they...he could rent a car to drive to the resort. She would be in the air, winging it back to San Diego. He was just hours away from saying goodbye to her.

Sympathy rushed through him for her, and he shoved it back. He wasn't going to endanger her no matter how much he understood why.

Her stiff back told him that she was renewing her anger all over again, and he couldn't blame her. He had lied to her as part of his mission. He'd had to say he would go along with her to get her to comply with his wishes and keep the arguments down to a minimum. That cupcake could argue the paint off the walls when she put her mind to it.

A formidable mind and a delectable body all wrapped up in enough attitude to fuel a metropolis.

Damn, why did he have to like her so much?

Trusting her, though. He wasn't so sure about that.

Outside of the SEALs, he'd had a lifetime of it shoved back in his face.

They went up an incline into the main part of the city, Dana leading the way. This would be the test to see if he could pass as her producer, Liam Nelson. They were similar, both of them with dark hair, and Ruckus was hoping the growth of beard would hide any dissimilar features.

But he suspected getting into Yaviza was much more difficult than getting into Panama City. They would just want to make sure people who were in the country had the correct traveling papers.

They entered an area where the buildings were small and without stilts, the muddy river down the hill.

"There is only one bus from Panama, and it should be here around noon, maybe sooner if the stops at the patrols along the way went smooth," she said. "We have time for a meal and some rest before it gets here. We can get tickets at the bus depot at the edge of town."

They stopped at the first cantina they came to for breakfast, then continued on to a light blue building that was a nice hotel. In their room, they dropped their packs and reclined on the bed. Dana turned her back to him. His attempt to try to help her must have backfired. She might have hung on to him in the small boat, but that was probably an any port in a storm thing.

Once again, he thought about the next step in this mission gone crazy. His simple tag and bag had turned into an odyssey, but he was determined to complete this assignment come hell, high water, or a cupcake.

After a couple hours of sleep and a quick combat wash, they were back out on the streets. At the bus depot, they bought their tickets. When a Senafront soldier asked for their papers, he presented Nelson's passport, which the distracted guard stamped and told them they were free to go.

They boarded the minivan that held about twenty-one people and made the short trip to Metiti, then transferred to an old school bus, the line called *Diablo Rojo*, Red Devil. After bumping over the road for hours on end with broken down shocks and squealing brakes, Ruckus was relieved to finally see Panama City in the distance. Gravel road gave way to a bumpy road, then smoothed out, the bus caught eventually in the stop-and-go traffic in Panama City. It was hard to believe that just hours away, the Gap existed in this bustling city, in a country that embraced technology and notorious for connecting oceans, cultures and world commerce.

This bus would drop them directly to Albrook International Airport, a gleaming modern terminal. There his guys would have already worked it out to rent a vehicle. They'd be on their way as soon as he got Dana on her flight.

As soon as they disembarked, he latched onto her pack to keep her close to him. Wicked had said the terminal was clear, but Ruckus knew that things on an op could turn on a dime. Her mouth tightened, and she shot him a nasty look.

Too bad, cupcake. They were doing this his way.

Right now, he needed to talk to his guys before he moved on.

He dragged her with him to a remote place in the airport. He inserted his earpiece and walked a few feet away from her.

"Ruckus to Rogue One, over."

"Copy, LT. We're here."

He kept his eyes on Dana. "Is the vehicle secure?"

"Yes, sir. Taken care of and the cupcake flight is in thirty minutes."

"Negate that," he said. He'd warred with his conscience and his duty. To himself, his country, and mostly, his team. They had a stake in this op, and if he was going to make this decision, they had to be one hundred percent on board because they believed in him, that his judgment was right and he'd make the best decision he could.

Back when he'd lied to her, his emotions weren't in the game. Dana Sorenson was nothing but a road bump to his HVT. Not a living, breathing woman who'd just supported him through some of the worst jungle he'd ever been in. She'd earned her chance at Salazar.

"Is everyone connected?" he asked.

"We're all here, LT. What's up?"

"Don't talk, just listen." Then he told them, all of it. Well, except the sex and all that kissing. Those things he left out. That was none of their goddamned business. But he knew they were hot-blooded American males and they could easily guess.

"If you think she should go, Boss," Kid said, "I'm in."

"Cowboy?" Ruckus said. "Be the judge, because I can't right now." He rubbed his forehead, agonizing over how to handle this. She was going to hate him if he put her on that plane. That was a given, but more importantly, she was going to be denied her closure and her due. That was even more damaging to his sense of justice.

"It's dangerous for her, sir," Cowboy said. "She's willing to risk her life for these memory cards?"

"She is determined."

There was a strained silence, then Cowboy said, "I think your decision is sound. She earned her spot. She had your back. I'm on board, too."

Blue, Wicked, Hollywood, Scarecrow, and Tank all voiced their agreement.

"Scarecrow, patch me through to the major." It only took him ten minutes to lay out his reasons for taking Dana, foremost that she would ease him into the resort, lessen suspicion, and she had a right to go after her memory cards. When he got the okay to proceed, he said, "Meet me at the vehicles, then. We're going in."

11

The terminal was thick with people either walking fast, milling around, or running full out for their flights. She maneuvered around people, the scents of food that made her mouth water and her stomach grumble, sheer bodies, and stairs as Bowie led her no doubt to her flight. She kept her head down, her anger growing with each step. The whole trip had been so mentally and physically exhausting, everything was catching up to her. In the distance, beyond the glass, the urban sprawl at the jungle's edge creating a haze in the air seemed almost surreal after the hard, harrowing trek. Her mind was on Bowie. He'd had such a hard childhood, and she could understand how everything he did had been dictated by the way he'd been betrayed by his parents.

But what he'd said to her was still reverberating deep inside. The guilt ebbing and flowing perhaps to the beginning of forgiveness. The dark thought that she may have stayed away on purpose, unable to bear the thought of her mother's passing, tortured her. Had she missed seeing her one last time because she couldn't handle it?

And had she pushed away her grief and invited in the guilt to make her suffering all that more poignant because she thought she deserved it? Had her mother and father's selfless life made it easy to transition into the one she led now? Barren and alone, even when she was in a relationship.

Everything she'd done after her mom's death, the travel, the less-than-perfect relationship, the inability to commit, the devastating stories was a way to alleviate her guilt. So remorseful, so isolated in her grief. Had she punished herself by denying her own happiness?

They haunted her, those words of his, because she was beginning to think he was right.

When they stopped, she looked up, but instead of the security checkpoint, it was the doors leading outside to the rental cars.

She shot him a startled look, but he was searching. She followed the direction of his stare. How could she have missed all that beefcake? Seven men standing around a black Hummer and a small sedan, Tank's dog Echo hanging out the window, his tongue lolling. And, my God, out of their uniforms, without their war paint, helmets, and all that freaking gear they carried, she realized that this was one gorgeous team. They hadn't gone unnoticed. Women were gawking. One woman walked into a pole, shook herself, and then moved on.

Ruckus, oblivious, moved through the glass doors and headed toward them. Hope started to build in her, hope that he had changed his mind.

They came to attention, the same kind of lethal focus she had seen in her SEAL many times. All she could think was "locked and loaded."

Two of the men she didn't recognize because they had

been "covering their backs," keeping their escape route open. The taller one looked menacing with his dark winged brows, but the crinkles beside his deep brown eyes made her think that he laughed often. The other one, Lord have mercy, was handsome as a movie star. "Wicked and Hollywood," Ruckus said as he introduced the two of them. They nodded to her, and she completely got their call names.

Wicked looked like a devil, and all Hollywood needed was adoring fans.

The others greeted her with a warm, new kind of respect, and there was only one way they would have known that she deserved it.

Bowie.

She turned to him, and he growled, "This is the way it's going down. The team is going to gear back up and head into the jungle outside of Santa Clara. You and I are going in as a couple to scope out the resort and find Salazar. Once we find him, we're going to call in the team and tag and bag him. Then we're going to get a chopper out of the airport. It's already been chartered."

She went to open her mouth.

But he cut her off. "You will do everything I say, when I say it. No arguments."

Kid smirked. "You can talk now. That's his I'm-ready-for-your-affirmative face."

The other guys chuckled, but she just stared at him, working to keep her emotions in check. She wanted to kiss him in the worst way, wrap her arms around him and just hold him. Instead, she nodded and said, "Copy that, sir."

That got more chuckles from the team and plenty of jealous looks from the passing women. She suddenly couldn't stop the tears as she turned away, opened the passenger side to the sedan, and slipped inside, surreptitiously wiping at her eyes. She felt like she was part of this team, and now, instead of going for something purely for herself, she was going to assist them in taking one of the most notorious wanted Americans in the world out of the international equation.

It wasn't long before the seven members of the team got into the Hummer. Ruckus settled into the sedan's driver's seat and started the car. Finally, she was going to get her memory cards and kick Salazar right where it hurt.

As he pulled out of the parking lot, she covered his hand where it rested against his big thigh. "Thank you," she said softly.

"Don't thank me," he said, "You earned it, cupcake." He turned right, and the Hummer went left. "We're going to the mall to shop. We need to look the part."

The mall was just as packed, and it almost seemed claustrophobic to her to have this many people in one space after the wilds of the Darién.

"I don't know the first thing about looking rich," he said wearily.

"Don't worry," she said. "I've got this covered. You go ahead and take care of the luggage, shoes, flip flops and a pair of deck shoes and the essentials you'll need. We'll have to smell the part as well as play the part. I'll meet you back here in about an hour. She looked at him and rattled off his measurements.

"That's right. How did you know that?"

"I shop for my dad. I'll see you in an hour."

She went to the men's shop and got him a few pairs of cotton shorts, a white button down with black palm trees, and a couple of polos, one in blue to match his eyes. She also picked out evening appropriate attire and figured he was a boxer brief kind of guy, controlled but loose, along with a pair of blue and white swim trunks. Just thinking about his lower body made her heart beat a little faster.

She got herself a couple of sundresses, shorts, and tops along with evening clothes, underthings, sandals, and flip flops. She chose cheap but expensive-looking jewelry. Then she went to the bath products store and indulged herself in some necessary nonessentials just because she wanted to smell like a girl.

With all that done, she beat him to the rendezvous. As soon as she saw him, it was evident to her that the women in Panama had really good taste. He was clueless to the female attention he was getting, and Dana couldn't help a little smirk of satisfaction that she'd had him, won the big, bad Navy SEAL over. He was now allowing her to finish out this Darién Gap trip with a win.

Not to mention the capacity he'd shown for compassion, tough compassion, but he'd opened her eyes to what she had been doing all these years. She wasn't quite sure how she was going to go back to her life without him in it. How she would change it to suit her new perspective. It was all so jumbled up and tangled now. Sorting through it would take some time. Hopefully, it would distract her from his absence in her life.

His intense gaze never left hers as he crossed the space that separated them. Her anger was gone, replaced with this gratitude. Would she always want more with this man?

"I found the food court."

"That's some amazing recon, sailor. Let's go."

He chuckled. "I'm sure you won't miss the fish heads and the rice."

"I don't like being watched *by my food* when I'm eating," she said with a laugh. "So, no. I won't miss Mr. Fish head or, for that matter, Mr. MRE either."

"Amen to that," he murmured.

After eating, they took the time to shove all their purchases into the two suitcases Ruckus bought, then took the sedan and stopped at the nearest hotel. She handled the room with her credit card and told him to go on up. She needed a couple more items she forgot. Heading to the shop, she ducked inside and bought what she needed.

RUCKUS WATCHED her disappear and felt just a twinge of worry. They were in a big city. There was no way the CLP would be hanging around a small hotel. She was safe.

Then he thought about what would happen if they both went up to the room together. He wasn't sure he could keep his hands off her.

Thirty minutes later he stepped out of a steaming shower, happy to be clean, but not feeling as rejuvenated as he hoped. He knew part of that was the anxiety he'd tried to ignore, quite unsuccessfully. Dana in danger. That was a hard one to get his mind around when he wanted the opposite.

She hadn't entered the bathroom, and he was supremely disappointed by that. Not that they had the time.

He stepped out the door and found Dana stretched out on the bed, fast asleep. And thought it was also one of the best feelings in the whole world. The relief was greater than it probably should have been, but he was human. She was fine. That was all that mattered to him right now.

His body, however, was even happier, if its reaction to seeing her all flushed and relaxed was any indication. In fact, it felt quite rejuvenated. Perhaps a cold shower would have done him more good.

He hated to wake her, but he was pretty sure she'd rather use what little time they had freshening up rather than sleeping. There would be time for that when they got to the resort. Time for other things as well. He was struck by how little he really knew her. And by how badly he wanted to correct that. It would take a lifetime to know everything about her, but they only had a few more days.

He wondered if he'd made the decision to allow her on the op because he just didn't want to put her on the plane and say goodbye. It was irrational. He was never irrational. Not when it came to missions. But getting involved with her in the field on an active op hadn't been his brightest idea.

He rubbed the towel over his hair, wondering what she'd bought him. He wasn't much of a clotheshorse. He glanced at her and smiled as he opened the case. She'd thought of everything. Badass, by-the-stars navigator, would-be wrestler of gators, and champion shopper.

"Why are you smiling? I hope you like what I picked out," she said, her voice all soft and drowsy with sleep.

He glanced at her in time to watch her stretch. His emotions were far too turbulent to deal with that temptation at the moment, so he turned and sat on the bed and started poking through the clothes. "I was thinking that if there was a prize for fastest shopper, you'd win hands down."

"I don't do things by halves, that's for sure." Her cheeks were a little rosy with sleep, her hair softly tangled around her face, her eyes a bit unfocused. And all he could think was that she struck him as the sort that called to him, quite strongly, to say the hell with clothes altogether and climb into the bed, right into her waiting arms, and into her warm and willing body. "It's amazing how you got my size perfect."

As if she was reading his mind, a provocative smile

curved her lips, sorely testing his willpower. "Oh, I think I know your size."

Yeah, fuck, he fit her perfectly, his dick deeply sheathed in all that slick warmth as tight as a glove.

He moved some soft fabrics and things lined with lace. Yeah, that stuff he didn't need to be fondling right now. At the bottom, he found a pair of men's shorts in tan. Opening the other suitcase, he found another pair of shorts, these ones black, and a blue polo. He pulled that out as well; then he saw the boxer briefs. She'd pegged him perfectly.

He held them up.

"Yeah, loose but controlled."

He chuckled. "You are something, cupcake."

She had slid to the edge of the bed. She yawned. "I hung up the evening stuff so it wouldn't get wrinkled."

"Evening stuff?"

"Yeah, you can't go in to dinner looking like a freaking commando." She tilted her head. "I think we did the rolling in the sheets part pretty good. The way I figure it, you at least owe me dinner."

He laughed. "Yeah, I'd say I at least owed you that. But, babe, I'm not exactly carrying around a wad of cash."

She blinked, then laughed. "Oh, right." She stood, then looked provocatively over her shoulder. "I guess with your performance, I can buy you dinner. But you'll owe me."

He stood, too, the big bed between them. *Stand tough, man*, he told himself.

"Yeah," he murmured. "I'll owe you."

She rummaged around in the case and skirted around him to the bathroom. It took his super SEAL control not to reach out, snag her, and toss her on the bed. He folded his arms across his chest to keep his hands out of harm's way.

He heard the shower go on and tried to block the mental

images that accompanied the sound. "Fuck me." Disgusted with his inability to get his head back on straight—and leave the other one out of it—he released the towel and tugged on the boxers. Then he pulled the polo over his head and donned the shorts, buttoning and zipping. Dressing in the clothes that she bought for him felt stupidly personal. Intimate, even. "You are such a goner," he muttered.

He raked his fingers through his drying hair and rubbed a hand across his chin. The growth of beard would have to go. He'd seen the clippers in the bag, but no razors. He tossed his old clothes into one of the pockets of the suitcase, then after another lingering look at the bathroom door, went to the balcony and contacted his team.

"Yeah, LT, we're in a holding pattern."

"Copy that."

"So Operation Cupcake Drop has turned into just plain Operation Cupcake?"

"I can see why you were persuaded, LT," Wicked said.

"Yeah," Hollywood agreed. "She's a freaking babe."

"Keep it in your pants, Hollywood. Anything that breathes and looks that good sets you on the prowl," Cowboy said.

"Hey, if she's up for grabs."

"Stop with the chatter," Ruckus said, not exactly jealous, but proprietary of Dana.

"Yeah, LT has dibs," Kid said.

Ruckus sighed. "Wipe that damn smug-ass grin off your face, Kid. The rest of you guys get your focus back on the mission. We're going to need to move fast once we have him."

"Yes, sir," Cowboy said.

After he cut off communication, he sat down and leaned his head back. He could use a twenty-minute power nap.

The next thing he knew, the sound of a door opening brought him fully awake. She was coming out of the bathroom. He blinked a few times, then slowly rose to his feet. He wasn't sure what he expected, but when she finally walked through the door, he knew he'd just been outclassed, outgunned, and outdone. All he could do was stand there and remember to keep his jaw off the floor.

This is what happened when this woman had thirty minutes to spruce up. She'd gone in looking wrinkled, dirty, mussed, and warm from bed, looking imminently edible. Now, she was dressed to kill, and he had to work not to be slain. She looked expensive and out of his league.

But what had made his jaw want to drop was the silky blonde hair. She was wearing a wig, and that made sense since Salazar knew what she looked like.

He liked her much better as a brunette.

She was wearing a red sundress that hugged every delectable curve. God help him to keep his hands off her. It covered her decently, but showed every dip and curve of her body, contours he wanted to run his hands all over.

She looked expensive, like red velvet with whipped cream and sprinkles, like come get me if you can, all wrapped up in a seductive package. Talk about a sweet cupcake.

She came toward him, shaking her head. "That won't do." Taking his hand, she drew him toward the bathroom, grabbing the clippers along the way.

She positioned him in front of the mirror, plugged in the appliance, and turned it on. She grabbed his chin, her brown eyes focused on what she was doing. But this close to her, he was surrounded by the most delicious smell to assault his nostrils. Damn, he wanted to drag her to the bed and bury his face in all that sweetness.

She sheared off the four days' growth of beard. "We want elegant," she murmured. She finished with the clippers, then reached into a bag on the toilet filled with girly stuff and pulled out a razor and small can of foam.

That's where she was keeping them.

She lathered his neck and set the razor against his throat, and he completely trusted her. The first stroke was clean and smooth. She turned, her neck looking so tantalizing as she swirled the razor in the small amount of water in the sink. When she turned back, he swore the bathroom had heated ten degrees. She took care of the rest of the hair there, then she reached for an aftershave, the citrus and sandalwood smell filling his nostrils. Hers flared. She smoothed it on his neck with a soft, gentle touch, then rubbed it over his stylish beard, her hands lingering. When she was done, they just stood there so close together, he could barely breathe.

He reached out and ran the backs of his fingers over her soft cheek. "You look amazing. Out of my league."

She shook her head, raising her hand again to touch his face, but he grabbed it and brought it to his mouth. "I wish we had more time," she whispered, her voice catching as he kissed her palm, the soft skin of her wrist.

"Me, too."

He let her go. They were on a timetable, and his team was waiting. They needed to get this show on the road. Once packed, they were moving at a good pace. The resort was located in Santa Clara, a beautiful Spanish-inspired place to indulge your every whim, the ocean a sparkling jewel in the distance. He pulled up to the circular drive of the resort. Several bellmen immediately moved in their direction.

He smiled at Dana. "Show time."

He could see the fatigue etched on her face quite clearly

now and knew he didn't look much better. But, before his eyes, she transformed. As the door opened, she offered her hand like a princess and the bellman took it, helping her out of the car.

Another one came around to the driver's side to take his car as he popped the trunk for their luggage.

She was moving toward the doors, a spring in her step, those white high-heeled sandals making her legs look a mile long.

He caught up to her and put his hand on her lower back as the bellman held the lobby door for them.

It was time to get the package they'd been sent to pick up. Nothing was going to stop him this time.

12

At the entrance to the dining room, he slipped her hand into the crook of his arm. This was actually kind of fun, pretending to be something she wasn't. The waiter showed them to their table, but the whole time she was looking for Salazar. From the moment they left their very beautiful and posh room, she'd been searching for him. All the trappings of this ruse aside, she'd like nothing better than to be on the beach with Bowie enjoying the ocean, the stars, and the delectable man beside her. Instead, she had poured herself into this dress that was tight in all the right places. She was a bit surprised at the fact that she'd lost some weight, the size smaller than what she normally wore. Maybe it was because she'd lost her appetite after her mom passed, or it could be running after a very fit SEAL through the jungle for hours on end with very little food.

Speaking of right places. Rough and tumble Ruckus cleaned up pretty damn well. He was in the white linen slacks, the loose, dark suitcoat, and the palm tree shirt looking elegant and expensive. She was a bit surprised at the amount of hair the navy allowed on their servicemen, but she guessed it was part and parcel of being special ops. He might have to do this kind of thing, go undercover, play many roles. Ruckus seemed as at home here in this elegant dining room as he did in the stronghold.

Apparently, Bowie made everything look good. He even made nothing look good. She'd say that nothing on him looked the best.

The waiter brought them to the table, and before he could hold her chair, Bowie was there, sliding it under her. That gentlemanly move made her a bit breathless. "The wine menu, *señor*."

"No wine," he said, his voice blunt. The waiter nodded and set menus in front of them. She picked up her water glass and took a sip, her eyes roaming the dining room. "I thought the red dress was spectacular, but the one you're wearing now, *hoo-yah* woman, you are something else.

She flashed him a grin and said, "I was just thinking the same thing about you, Lieutenant."

He reached out and took her hand, bringing it to his mouth, kissing her fingers in a show of affection. It might be a cover, but oh boy, his lips were so soft, his breath warm against her knuckles.

"You have pretty hands," he murmured.

She looked down at her menu, and her stomach rumbled at the thought of eating a solid meal. The waiter came back, and they ordered, playing the loving couple to a T. She went for the surf and turf and Bowie ordered a filet mignon.

As she handed the menu to the waiter, she saw Salazar walk into the dining room, a Latin beauty on his arm. A shiver went down her spine at the man who had kidnapped her, controlled her for two weeks, who had terrorized her crewmembers. The man who had been much too familiar with her as if any woman in his orbit was fair game.

She hadn't mentioned Salazar's appetites to Bowie because she had no intention of ever being under the man's power again. They were going neutralize him, and she'd get her memory cards. After that, it was back home to edit her project and get it ready for broadcast. She and Bowie would go their separate ways.

She didn't even have to say a thing to him. He already knew by her posture that she'd spotted him. "Relax," he murmured, and she let her stiff shoulders go. "That's better. Now smile for me, Dana." She met his eyes, and it was easy to smile into the blue depths. "There you go. We don't have a care in the world here. We're on vacation." She nodded. "We'll enjoy our meal, and when he's done, we'll follow them. Get the lay of the land and where his room is. Once that's accomplished, you're going to get very demanding and get us as close to him as possible."

"All right. I can be pretty bitchy."

"I know."

"Hey," she said, giving him a bitchy look.

He chuckled. "Yeah, just like that, cupcake. That will do it."

They lingered over dinner, and she even ordered dessert, loving every bite. The minute that Salazar and his lady love rose from the table, she and Bowie rose, too.

Instead of heading back up to their room, they strolled to the back of the hotel. "They're going for a moonlight walk. That's going to be pretty conspicuous if we go, too," she said.

"No, it won't. It'll be natural. We'll keep an eye on them and spend some time on lovey dovey crap."

"You're so romantic," she groused as they pushed

through the door, his arm around her holding her close to his hard body.

His eyes were on Salazar, but he said, "You have no idea how good I am in the romance department, sweetheart."

"I think I have some idea how you are on the hot and heavy part."

"Between the sheets stuff is easy," he said taking her hand and pulling her down off the patio onto the sand. "It's romance that's hard." Salazar and his partner kept moving. Bowie reached down and removed his shoes, setting them beneath a table with an umbrella. She reached for his shoulder for balance as she slipped off her sandals. He caught her around the waist, anchoring her.

Startled, she looked at him, but he was in SEAL mode, preoccupied with tracking Salazar. Suddenly, she wanted him in a normal setting, a real date, something that was mundane and everyday instead of this tension and danger every minute.

They followed at a distance, and it was easy to get caught up in the night, the stars brightening the sky with tiny twinkles, the soft lapping of the ocean waves, the gentle breeze, and the deep, abiding attraction she had for this man.

Salazar stopped and pulled the woman against him. Bowie back-walked her over to an outcropping of rock. "You know that scent you're wearing is very distracting," he murmured. "I don't usually have many tantalizing scents around me when I'm working with those knuckleheads. They don't smell as good as you do."

She giggled. "Your job is so tough. Having to hang around with all those macho guys all the time, giving orders. It must be so darn taxing."

He gave her a long-suffering sigh. "It is, and every one of

them is as confident as all get out and smart asses to boot, especially Kid."

He said the young man's name with so much affection, it was easy to see that he loved his team. Why not? He'd been in the navy a long time, and after what he'd gone through as a teenager, it was easy to understand how much they meant to him.

With them, it did feel like a band of brothers.

Hooking his thumb under her jaw, he tipped her head and brushed his mouth against hers. "I find that this has to be one of my favorite clusterfucks ever."

She laughed. "You've got to be kidding. Let me see: running through the jungle, people trying to kill us, gunfire, people trying to kill us, things blowing up, *people trying to kill us*, wrestling alligators—" At his expression, she said, "Oh, excuse me, caiman, and dealing with a woman who was arguing with you all the way. I believe you wanted to throttle me more than once."

"People are always trying to kill me. Nothing new. I just try to make sure I take them out first. But, yeah, best damn op ever. I found a way to shut you up."

He covered her mouth in a hot, wet kiss, and she relinquished conscious thought. All she could do was hang on to the one solid thing in her spiraling universe.

His touch dragged her down, deeper, and she slipped her arms around his neck, pressing tighter. "That's an effective maneuver, Lieutenant. But I think it works both ways."

Ruckus grinned and gave her a hard hug. "I'm going to keep my thoughts to myself on that one."

"Oh, your body is telling the truth."

"What can I say? I'm a man and you affect me, cupcake, all the way around, especially in that dress." He ran his thumb along her cheekbone. "And out of it."

She looked up at him, her heart skipping a beat when she saw the dark, unsmiling expression in his eyes. He held her gaze a split second; then he lowered his head. Snagging her chin, he brushed her mouth with the softest, slowest kiss. Dana's breath caught, and her pulse stumbled. His lips moving against hers, he said, his voice very low, very raspy, "We'd better follow them before I forget why we're here."

It looked like Salazar was finally moving toward the hotel, and hand-in-hand, they followed them. They retraced their steps and picked up their shoes, going back into the hotel. At the elevators, she used his shoulder to hide her face while they got in and watched as the elevator climbed. When it stopped on the seventh floor, Ruckus looked at Dana. "Let's get your bitchy act on and get us to the seventh floor. It's getting late. We need get some sleep, and we can stake it out tomorrow to find out exactly what room they're in. Once we get that info, we can then get inside and search it. We'll get the chance to also search him if the cards aren't inside the room.

She nodded, her pulse skittering thinking about being alone with Bowie again.

They headed toward the front desk and she made such a stink, the hotel reassigned them to the seventh floor. As they changed rooms, the tension between them tightened. It occurred to her that there could be repercussions regarding her involvement in this op. "So, your boss, what does he think about me being here?"

"Other than the fact that you're being exposed to danger, he was all for you being the buffer. Because we want to keep this hush-hush. Get him and then get out of the country with no one the wiser. It requires a little more finesse than we normally worry about."

"That's a relief. I don't want you to be in trouble for my

determination to get my work back, since it was my decision to do this."

Inside the door, he grabbed her around the waist and pressed her against the wall. "Actually," she said breathlessly. "It was your decision, and you allowed me to come along, convincing your superiors that I was important. This could have ended badly."

"It still could, Dana. This is a snatch and grab, and there's never anything set in stone. But I will do everything in my power to get your memory cards back and make sure you're safe. That's a promise," he said, his voice rough.

"I trust you will," she said.

"Cupcake? I know the cards are important to you because of what's on them, but do you think that you could be missing something here?"

"What's that?"

"You didn't get a chance to say goodbye to your mom. Now you have something that she wanted you to do that was full of time, effort, and professionalism. A story to be told. But maybe what this whole Darién Gap trip is giving you is closure. Did you allow yourself to grieve her?"

Dana was taken aback by his words. Closure? Was that even possible? Could she honestly say that she had allowed herself to grieve her mom, or had she been punishing herself for the guilt all this time? Her mom had been such an amazing role model, selfless, courageous, even in the face of death, dauntless. Had Dana sacrificed too much of her life to be constantly at risk as a war correspondent, then undertaking these dangerous journeys into hazardous parts of the world just to be the woman her parents would be proud of? Had her mother been proud of her? She knew deep in her heart that her mom loved her. That was an unequivocal certainty. But had she been proud of her? She squeezed her eyes closed.

His breath was warm against her neck as he pressed his face against hers. "Hey, it's okay," he whispered, his voice husky. Then he so gently angled her away from him, and he looked into her eyes. His gaze was so electric that Dana jerked away from him, but he pulled her back. "You made me open my eyes, sweetheart. You made me think about my own life. What I want. Who I am. Who I could be." He tightened his arm around her shoulders when she tried to bolt again, get away from his words. "I wanted to make sure you were doing all this for the right reasons, not under some misconception about what you really wanted. I think it's better to be informed."

Beginning to tremble, Dana buried her face in his neck, trying to get her mind around what he'd said. Then Bowie grabbed her chin.

"I don't know," she said, unable to actually verbalize what she thought at this point because she was now in mental turmoil. "I can't think around you. This is something. More than I had ever thought possible."

"It's something, babe. I can't deny that. We've been through some stuff here."

"It's not that. It's more than that and you know it. Connection, Bowie."

"Dana..." he said, his voice subdued.

But she didn't want to do this now. She wasn't ready to define what they had. She knew it was substantial, but Bowie was a SEAL. He had his own crap going on. It seemed complicated.

"Let's not do this now," she whispered.

"All right," he answered. Hooking his thumb under her jaw, he tipped her head and brushed his mouth against hers, telling her exactly what he wanted to do and how he was going to do it. His explicitness made her breathless, her breathing ragged, and everything that seemed complicated and important tumbled right out of her head. She hung on to him, feeling as if she was about to dissolve.

He took, but he gave so much. She gripped his arm, her senses spinning out of control. He tightened his hold, his voice rough and ragged against her ear as he urged her on. Kissing her, his mouth ravenous, he pushed her toward the bed. He reached under the dress, drawing her hips hard against his groin. He delved into the waistband of her panties, cupping her bare ass. Then, impatiently, he pulled the dress over her head, the flounced skirt landing in a heap on the floor. She could barely breathe, anticipating loving this man. Her heart contracting because that word did have a heavy meaning here.

"Jesus, Dana," he whispered, removing her bra. His mouth slid along her skin, destroying her, creating a tempest inside her that could only be quenched by this man.

He cupped her breasts, kneading them, his thumbs brushing over the nipples. His head dipped, and he captured one of her nipples. She cried out and arched her back as he sucked and laved the hard tip.

His hand delved into her panties, touching her hot, swollen flesh, finding the sweet spot and relentlessly massaging it with his frantic touch. Everything tightened. He was so in tune with her body, playing her like a master until all that burgeoning need started to pull tighter and narrow, and with one last stroke, he took her over the top. She stiffened and sobbed out his name as the paralyzing release ripped through her, turning her into raw, exploding energy.

He pushed her back onto the bed and stripped off her underwear. Then he removed his clothes in a flurry of movement, baring his sleek, heavy muscles before he pushed her legs open for the heat of his cock to enter her in one thick, heavy move. He moaned deeply in his chest as she gasped at the first delicious feel of him filling her.

"Bowie, oh please," she whispered as he pulled out and shoved in again, capturing her leg and hooking it up with his shoulder so that he could get deeper, closer, thrust harder. "*Bowie.*"

Immobilized by the onslaught of need, Dana clung to him, certain she was never going to get enough of this man, and it saddened her that she had spent so much of her life without this...this passion. He fit to her like they were made for each other, like a puzzle piece she'd been searching for and had never found. Everything about him was so dynamic, the way he fought, felt, spoke, fucked her. It was all so wonderful, the raw emotion stunning her.

Her breathing out of control, she locked her arms around him, his harsh breath and sounds of pleasure rolling over her. His mouth devoured hers even as he took her body over and over again. Hoarsely whispering her name, he slipped his hand around her throat in such a sexy, possessive move, she arched into him, his thrusts getting deeper, sweat pouring off his body. She lifted herself to meet him as he caressed her throat, his hand so big he almost encircled the circumference. His hips moved as he thrust his head back. "Dana, babe," he pleaded. "Come for me. Let go."

This madness gripped her, and she knew that this trip had changed her, this man had changed her, ruined her, remade her in this fire and heat. Making a low sound of surrender, he buried his face in her neck, kneeling over her, grasping her legs and thrusting hard and fast. His breathing raw and labored, he kissed down her neck, took one of her nipples in his mouth, and sucked her hard.

She could barely catch her breath.

Her whole life had been about giving back, reporting responsibly. She'd come out here to find a heartbreaking truth. Little did she know that the truth she would find would blow her world to smithereens, and she'd found this man. This magnificent man who'd had the decency, the compassion to listen to her, understand what she needed, and had given her not only the gift of himself, but the golden opportunity to bring everything she'd worked for to fruition. She couldn't even think about what her life would have been without him in it. What would have happened, how she would have ignored the signs and the messages that were trapped in her mind. Her refusal to see that she had been sacrificing everything. *Everything.*

He'd opened her eyes to her own deep, dark truth, something that she hadn't wanted to face, but that he believed she had the courage to recognize.

For that she would always be grateful to him.

Unsure how it would change her world, and what she would do once this was all over, she clung to him with all she had.

When he raised his head and their eyes met, she couldn't breathe. There was so much raw emotion, so much agony of pleasure, pain, need there. She cupped his face, then brought his mouth down to hers so she could do her best to alleviate it. This beautiful man who had given Dana her mom back.

Her voice catching on a sob, she whispered his name and the aching returned. Blinded by sensation, she arched into his thrusts, giving him as much as she could, feeling fused from two halves into one whole. Every thrust sent her higher and higher until her whole body exploded into a white-hot light, then everything exploded again, pulses of relief ripping through her, a million lights going off in her head. And on a tortured groan, Bowie twisted his hips, his own release pumping into her.

Incoherent and shattered, she hung on to him for dear life—on to her warrior, her Ruckus, her strong center.

It seemed like an eternity before bits of consciousness returned. His body heavy on hers, the weight of him, warm and solid, made her sigh softly against his skin. Trembling and weak, and feeling as if every bone in her body had been liquefied, she wrapped her arms around him, aware of how tightly he was holding her, aware of how badly he was shaking.

Tears stung her eyes, tears of release and compassion, and the feeling that there would never be anything like this in her life ever again. That Bowie was so special, so precious that she couldn't get her mind around not trying to see where this went. But it took two people to move forward, and she wasn't sure he was willing to go that far. What if she put herself out there and he didn't accept? She bit her lip.

He had his own painful loose ends to tie up as well. Not to mention he would have to finish out this op and get Salazar transported where he needed to go. A relationship with a SEAL wouldn't be easy, and how much would her life have to change to accommodate him?

Bowie turned his face against her neck, his hand wedged under her head. Then as if too spent to move, he tightened his hold. "I can feel you thinking really hard," he said gruffly. "I think I'm offended."

"Offended?"

"Yeah, I can't put two coherent sentences together. I don't want you to either."

Bracing his weight on his elbows, he lifted his head and gazed down at her, the moonlight washing over his features. Taking her face in his hands, he studied her, a slow smile appearing. His voice was like rough velvet when he spoke. "Ah, Dana, my cupcake. You are full of surprises."

Holding back a grin, she reached up and caressed his mouth. "You have a few surprises yourself, Bowie."

His smile deepened. "You're a little piece of dynamite, you know that?"

She did grin. "Did I blow you to smithereens?"

He laughed, a low throaty laugh that sent delicious shivers up her spine. "Something like that."

Aware that they were both avoiding what had brought them together, Dana raised her head and kissed him along his jaw. It was almost as if they'd silently struck another pact not to open too many doors, and that was okay. This was too special to risk. Wanting to keep that comfortable easiness between them, she looped her arms around his neck and gave him another grin. She didn't know why, but she wanted to see if she could make him blush. Keeping her voice deliberately provocative, she murmured, "You're very, very good, Lieutenant Cooper."

His expression altered, and even in the faint moonlight filtering in, she could see his eyes darken, his gaze becoming hot and intimate. He stroked her cheeks with his thumbs, then lowered his head, brushing his mouth lightly against hers. "Oh, yeah," he breathed, caressing her bottom lip. "You better find some handholds, babe, because this is going to get rough."

With that gravely uttered sentence, Dana's heart started stammering, and her body went into overload.

She pulled his head down and brought his mouth into full contact with hers. The kiss was slow, soft, and so unbelievably gentle, and her whole body turned to jelly. A sudden urgency sizzled through her, and she locked her arms around him, lifting her hips to urge him on. Dragging both her arms from around his neck, he laced his fingers through hers, holding her hands against the bed.

"Easy, darlin'," he whispered, moistening her bottom lip with the tip of her tongue. "We're going to take our time— slow and easy." He stroked her palms with his thumbs and shifted ever so gently against her. "This time we're going to make it last." Dana's heart nearly climbed right out of her chest. She didn't think she could stand it. She really didn't. He'd only started, and it was too much already.

And Bowie did take his time—goodness, did he take his time. It was just like the kiss, slow, soft, gentle. And painstakingly thorough—inch by inch. Dana had no idea a man could be that dedicated to detail, and he set off reactions she'd never, ever experienced before. And she couldn't think of anything, except what he was doing to her. He took it so slow and easy, he nearly drove her crazy, and she was practically clawing at the bedding before he gave in to her. She was sure she was on the verge of losing her mind when he finally thrust into her, driving her up and over into a soul-shredding release. It was so unbelievable, so explosive, it was as if she came right out of her body. And he was the only thing that held her together. But then, he had been there to hold her together from the beginning.

Everything about him spoke to her. The words as beautiful as the way his body moved.

And she wanted this, always.

Always. Always. Always.

13

When Ruckus opened his eyes the next morning, he and Dana were tangled up in the sheets and in each other. His heart simply turned over when he looked at her. This was the strangest op he'd ever been on. Last night had been wild and full of her luscious skin and soft cries. They were hours away from the completion of his mission. As soon as Salazar was in custody, she would be getting on a plane back to San Diego.

He immediately rejected that thought. He didn't want to be one inch away from her let alone thousands of miles. But this was it. The end of the road for both of them. This wild journey through the jungle that had dumped them into paradise at the outskirts of Panama City was over. He didn't want to think about this anymore. He didn't want to ache like this, and he certainly didn't want to say anything he would regret. He wasn't the in-the-heat-of-the-moment guy, and he never admitted to anything first. He needed that safety net.

The major had made it clear. She could accompany him as soon as they had Salazar bagged, but then after a quick debrief, she would be out of SEAL and navy business. He slipped out of bed and into the shower. Dressing in dark pants and a T-shirt, he layered the palm tree shirt over it, he checked the pistol, racked the slide, and chambered a round. He tucked his sidearm into the holster at the small of his back. Salazar was traveling with bodyguards, but Ruckus was sure he could take them out.

He smiled softly thinking about Dana in the tent, her hand around the grip. How she had proudly said that she knew a round was a bullet.

He braced his back against the bathroom door and took her in, his gaze sliding up from the tips of her delicate toes to those rounded calves, to the long stretch of mouth-watering leg, to the nipped in slender waist, over the beautiful globe of a breast tipped with a blush pink nipple, a column of pretty neck to the features of her arresting face.

Her dark hair was a tousled, tangled mess, and his hands itched to bury themselves in the silky mass. Damn, but his heart ached all over again.

He hoped that she heard his words about her mom. She was too much of a vibrant person to give up so much of her life to slog around in the muck and nastiness of the dark side of the world. She ought to think about being happy. That's what he wanted for her.

But what did he want for himself? What was his next step now that she had opened his eyes about his dad and how his hatred, resentment, and inability to forgive him kept him shackled?

But how could he forgive the man who had made him into what he was today? Scarred, wrecked, damaged inside. He'd been incapable of letting go of any of that in his past. Yet, his relationship with Dana was solid. He was lost in this woman and had no idea how to get himself out, to save himself.

Not even sure he wanted to be saved at all.

She stirred, and he moved back to the bed. She opened her eyes and turned her head, automatically seeking him. Reaching out, she wrapped her hand around his wrist. "You're already locked and loaded?"

"You know it, babe. It's end game time, and I want you to get yourself dolled up. We're going to discover where his room is. You up for that?"

She sat up, leaving her body bare to his eyes, and he ran his hands over her before he could stop himself. She made a soft sound and, on her knees, walked across the mattress and into his arms. He held her, stroking down her spine, the skin of her back soft, the muscles beneath firm.

"How can I not want this to end?" she whispered. "It's been one of the most harrowing times of my life. I should want to go home."

He closed his eyes and crushed her closer. "Don't. We both know how this is going to end. There's no need to make it any harder than it is."

She reared back and looked him in the eyes for a long minute. "It is hard, isn't it, Bowie?"

"Yes," he ground out as he kissed her mouth, squeezing his eyes tightly closed.

She clung to him, and he held her tenderly, his heart feeling ripped from his chest. This was so damned unexpected. After Mary Jo, he had vowed he couldn't do this to himself again. He had been the worst husband, a bastard of a partner. He'd hurt her, and he realized that now. Hurt her hard with his inability to open himself up to even the smallest chance that he could get hurt. With Dana, she terrified him, and he couldn't shake the feeling that he really was that person, the one who couldn't sustain any type of relationship outside the SEALs.

Was he falling for this woman? He was pretty sure he was. She was a dynamo, brave, smart, resourceful, fit, and kept up with him. There weren't many women who would have reacted the way she had out there in the jungle. Not when he'd had to take down all those CLP guys and when he'd had to cross that river twice, fight alligators, fight for their lives.

He wanted her, but it was completely impossible.

So he took his time, tenderly holding her naked body against him, generating memories of her that he could revisit when he needed something good in his life to remember. There was no way he could ever forget her.

He let her go and said softly, "Get going, babe. We have a mission to complete." He slapped her on her shapely butt as she slipped off the bed and sauntered her sexy-ass beauty into the bathroom and closed the door.

His dick was hard as a rock, but he wasn't going to act on his baser needs. The sex was nothing compared to her smart mouth and her even smarter brain. He wanted more for her, and he just wasn't enough.

She deserved more.

After she came out dressed in a pair of white capri pants and a flowered top, the wig firmly in place, he took her arm and they exited the hotel room. They would be checking out today. All he had to do was get Salazar out of here, down to the parking deck, and into the trunk of the sedan where he would call in his team. They would all rendezvous at the airport and take their chartered flight back to the *Annenberg*. Dana would come with them for a quick debrief, and then she would be free to go back to San Diego.

It was about eight when they exited their room. This was

when breakfast dishes would most likely either be delivered or picked up. Housekeeping was at the head of the hall.

"If you spot him, note the room and keep on walking. Be careful."

"Yes, Dad. I'll be extra careful."

"Smart-ass," he growled.

Dana walked one way and he walked the other. She was so natural at this he wondered if she was even minutely scared.

As he walked, people were emerging from their rooms, some dressed for the beach or pool, some for a day of shopping, others looking like they were going for a late breakfast or brunch.

By the time he got to the end of the hallway, it was clear that either Salazar hadn't emerged or that he was in Dana's territory.

When he turned a corner, he spied her walking briskly toward him. "I found him. A big guy in a black suit set the breakfast dishes outside." She named the room and they walked briskly toward it. She looked at him, and he pulled out his weapon, then nodded. "Housekeeping," she said. A few moments later, the door opened, and Ruckus shoved the gun in the man's face while Dana put the "Do Not Disturb" sign on the door as it closed behind them.

He pulled back his fist and slammed it into the man's face. He flew backwards into the wall, slid down, and was still. Another bodyguard came out of the suite, and Ruckus brandished his weapon. The man stopped in his tracks. With the butt end of the gun, he took care of him, and he was also down for the count.

"What is going on out there?"

At the sound of Salazar's voice, Dana stiffened.

"What is the meaning of—"

"Shut up," Ruckus said as Salazar took in his unconscious bodyguards. His attention swung to Ruckus.

Before he could say anything, Dana pulled off the wig and shoved Salazar in the chest. "Where are my memory cards, you son of a bitch?"

"Dana," he said, his voice way too familiar, the purr of it putting Ruckus on edge.

Ruckus flex-cuffed the two guards and they all crowded into Salazar's bedroom.

Salazar watched Dana much too closely as she rummaged through his things. "I'd be happy to return them to you if you'd accompany me back to the stronghold."

She turned and hissed at him, "I wouldn't go across the street with you. Where are they?"

"In a safe place," he murmured.

She cried out in frustration, but he only smirked, not seeming at all worried. "Can you search him?" she asked Ruckus, and he realized that she was afraid of him, of touching him. A kernel of anger flared inside him.

Salazar's focus switched to Ruckus, and his eyes narrowed. "Ah, she had her own personal hero. Special ops, I'd presume. SEAL?"

Ruckus didn't respond, just handed Dana the gun and walked up to the bastard and searched his body.

He turned to her, and her face twisted in anger and disgust. Before he could stop her, she shoved the gun into Salazar's face. "Where are they? I want them back."

He stood close to her, understood now why she was acting this way, confronting this man who had terrorized her. "Easy," he said, wrapping his hand around hers on the grip.

"You're not going to kill me, Dana. You don't have it in you to shoot an unarmed man in cold blood."

She stared at him, the underlying fear of him making her edgy. With a soft cry, she relinquished the gun to Ruckus and turned away, working on composing herself.

Ruckus put the gun back up to Salazar's face. "She might not kill you in cold blood, Salazar, but I, on the other hand, won't have a problem. I'll sleep like a baby tonight dreaming of castles in the sky and unicorns."

For the first time since he'd entered the room, Salazar blinked. He glanced over at Dana and then back at him. "Ah, so that's the way it goes. How is she? After I've had her, we should compare notes."

Ruckus knew this ploy, and he wasn't going to rise to the bait. He pressed the muzzle of the pistol to his head and gave it another small push. "Time is running out."

Salazar looked into Ruckus's eyes and his widened slightly, then his mouth tightened. "All right. They're at my stronghold. We'll have to go back there."

Dana made a soft, distressed sound and turned to look at Ruckus. "Not on your life, Salazar. You have a one-way ticket to DC. There's a chopper waiting at the airport. That's where you're going."

Salazar gave Dana a mock apologetic look and said, "Sorry, babe, looks like you lose."

She marched up to him and slapped him across the face.

Ruckus looked at his watch. "We've got to move." He grabbed Salazar's arm and dragged him to the front door. "If you so much as peep, you're going to be the first one to die."

"I'm a busy man. I don't have time for this," he said nonchalantly as if he were talking to his secretary.

Ruckus put the gun in his back and they exited the room. At the elevator, Dana pushed the button for the garage. It came up empty, and they got inside. As it started to descend, Salazar reached out and slid his finger down her arm. She jerked away, her eyes filled with anger and revulsion.

Salazar just laughed. Ruckus wanted just five minutes with this guy to tune him up. Everything from his childhood rose up, and he grabbed Salazar's neck and pinned him to the back of the elevator, his hand tightening until Salazar's face went red.

"No, don't. It's not worth it. He's just pushing your buttons. That's what he does."

Breathing hard, Ruckus backed off and with one slam of his hand against the wall, he eyed Salazar. "Don't touch her again."

When the elevator dinged at the garage level, Ruckus shoved Salazar out into the humid air, smelling of gasoline, rubber and exhaust fumes. He stumbled a bit and then righted himself. Adjusting his suit coat, he gave Ruckus a nasty look.

Ruckus shoved him again, and he started moving toward the sedan. The comm in his ear came to life.

"LT? We on track?"

"Yeah, package is secured. Rendezvous in ten."

"Copy that."

They snaked among the cars until they made it to the sedan. Ruckus pushed the key lock and the trunk lid popped open.

Then someone shouted, "Salazar! Where the hell are you going?"

It was Nunez, and it looked like he had the buyers with him. He was walking away from a black SUV with several other men. As soon as they saw Ruckus's gun, they were reaching for their own. Gunfire erupted. Ruckus grabbed Dana's arm and dragged her behind the car as bullets peppered the vehicles around them. The back windshield shattered, raining glass all over them.

"We're under fire," he screamed into the mic. Get your asses here, now. Salazar is in the wind."

"We're on our way, LT. Hang on."

Automatic weapons against a nine mil wasn't going to cut it, but his M4 was still disassembled in the pack in the back seat of the car along with their suitcases and Dana's pack. He needed his team and their firepower yesterday.

"Come on, guys!" He turned to find Dana looking crestfallen and angry at the same time. Fear made her eyes wide. He popped up and returned fire.

"We can't let him get away." She slipped away from him and disappeared around the front of the car.

"Dana," he hissed. "No!"

"Be advised, cupcake in the line of fire. Cupcake in the line of fire." Son of a bitch! He couldn't lose her. He should be concerned about bagging his HVT, but he couldn't care less about the guy right now. He wanted Dana out of immediate danger. He moved and saw that she had Salazar in sight. He was crouching behind a car. It wouldn't be long before he would run to his buyer buddies and this was going to get even uglier.

When Salazar went to take off, she tackled him to the pavement, slamming his face into the concrete.

He came up behind her and pulled her off, grabbing Salazar by the arm and dragging him up from the ground. He forced him behind a bank of cars and said, "If you run again, I'll put a bullet in you."

Then someone ran around one of the cars, and before Ruckus could return fire, the guy pulled the trigger. Ruckus jumped in front of Dana and a bullet slammed into his arm. Then Salazar grabbed her and shouted, "Kill him!"

Salazar pulled her with him as the armed guy turned to him. He had him dead to rights, and there was no way he could raise his wounded arm in time to kill him.

Then the sound of a vehicle's heavy engine roared into the garage, and the vehicle slammed into the guy. Ruckus's gut clenched, and he pushed up off the ground as Kid in full battle dress came running over. "LT's been hit."

"Don't worry about me. Dana," he said.

Cowboy helped him up, and they hustled him over to the vehicle as sirens sounded in the distance. The cops couldn't catch them. "Go," he said.

"Where?"

"The airport. He knows we have the chopper there. Fast."

As Tank put the Hummer into gear, he said, "Hang on." He drove out of the parking garage and made a sharp left onto the highway while Blue ripped his sleeve and tended to his wound. "A through and through," he said.

Ruckus didn't give a damn about his arm or Salazar. He wanted Dana back.

Kid, his face shadowed, in full SEAL mode, growled, "We're getting her back and we're getting Salazar. No matter what it takes."

"*Hoo-yah!*" Tank said, hitting the gas as the Hummer jumped into a higher speed. Scarecrow, Wicked, and the rest of them murmured their affirmatives. Ruckus couldn't imagine a better damn team to go in and get her out of there. He had no illusions that Salazar wouldn't go back to his stronghold, his little slice of American pie, and his gut clenched. Salazar wanted Dana. He wanted her against her will. The bastard fed on a woman's fear, and everything from his childhood rushed up like an oily, sick wave of despair. God, he'd hated his father, and that anger had fueled him for so many years. How could he let it go? It seemed to be a part of him, what ran his machine. Would he even be an effective SEAL without it? Could he let it go, and would it be the best thing for him?

Being a SEAL was the only thing he'd ever done right, up until right now. He'd let her down, hadn't been able to deliver her memory cards to her. Salazar was most likely lying to her.

The Hummer hit the airport, and Tank stopped at the gate. He'd already received clearance. The guard eyed them but let them through.

When they pulled up, Salazar and his group of thugs were running for the chopper with Dana in tow. She was fighting every step of the way until Salazar punched her in the face and she went limp.

Ruckus roared and broke into an all-out sprint, but the rotor blades were already turning and Nunez opened fire. Cowboy hit Ruckus from behind, taking him down, avoiding the barrage of bullets whizzing in the heated air.

When he looked up, he saw Dana's pale face, her eyes closed and slumped over Salazar's lap. He laughed and pointed an imaginary gun at Ruckus and pulled the trigger. Ruckus shook Cowboy off and was up and running again, but it was too late. As his gut churned, the chopper lifted up into the impossibly blue sky, banking to the left. The pilot gunned the engine, and it shot off toward the jungle, back into the Darién Gap.

Ruckus just stared at the disappearing bird. This couldn't be happening. He could do unspeakable things to her before Ruckus could get there in time. Then rotors beating the air sounded behind him. When he whipped around, Kid was in the driver's seat. He set the bird down.

"Need a lift?" he shouted, and all the SEALs grabbed the

gear and packs out of the Hummer and sedan, piling inside. Tank muscled Kid over.

Tank said, "I'll fly it. I don't trust you to make a straight line. No loop-de-loops for us."

"Hey, we've got a babe to save and a package to deliver. I know my priorities."

"Where did you get this bird?"

"It was just hanging around, fully fueled, and we're just borrowing it, right? No harm in a little borrow."

Blue shook his head. "It's outright stealing, Kid. Good job!"

Ruckus's attention was on Dana. He had to get to her before it was too late. The chopper whizzed over the trees, Tank's sure, confident hands guiding the controls. "Where do you want to put down, LT? That place is going to be crawling with tangos. We've got our work cut out for us."

"As close as possible, Tank. It's not going to be a secret we're coming. But I'm not leaving without her."

"And the package," Scarecrow said, his report to the brass shouted into the radio.

Ruckus's eyes narrowed, and he let out a breath.

"Oh, damn, some shit is going to go down," Kid said. "Maybe you should let us handle the package."

"Sure," Ruckus said. "You can pick up the pieces after I'm done with him."

All the guys exchanged glances. Their mission from the beginning had been to secure Salazar, bring him to the *Annenberg*, get him to DC. Get justice for the men and women he'd killed. But he'd lost that perspective. Dana was all that was important to him at this point. Much more important than a drug-dealing, murdering scum. He would save her. He had to save her.

He didn't want to analyze why because that would be

counterproductive. He just knew that he wouldn't survive if something happened to her. He didn't want to survive.

He'd use all his training, all his skills, all his authority to make it happen. If he was too late, Salazar would irreparably hurt Dana. She'd never be the same woman. She'd be broken, bitter, scarred just like him, and he couldn't bear it.

The chopper flew over the stronghold, the men below them looking up. Cowboy fired up the 50 cal, and they all scattered. They were coming in hot, and there was no way he was leaving without her.

No goddamned way.

14

Dana came awake with a start and sat up in the bed she'd occupied when he'd kept her captive.

Her head was throbbing, her jaw hurt, and she tasted blood in her mouth. The bastard had hit her. She got up, rushed over to the door, and tried the handle, but to her horror, it was locked.

Her thoughts immediately went to Bowie. He'd been shot. To protect her, he'd thrown his body in front of hers. Tears filled her eyes, her fear for him twisting like a knife in her gut. If anything happened to him because she was so hell-bent on getting her memory cards, she would never forgive herself.

That was the crux of her problem as she ran to the window and looked out. The compound was full of men, all armed. Her heart sank.

She backed up, tears running down her cheeks at the memory of loving Bowie and the way he'd treated her, so roughly gentle. Her throat got tight.

She was in love with him.

"Oh, God," she sobbed. She had to get out of here

because no matter what, SEAL Team Alpha was coming for her. There was no doubt in her mind.

Then she heard the door and knew what was coming. She'd known ever since that hood had been snatched off her head that the moment Salazar was finished waiting, he would force her.

She looked frantically around for a weapon, but there was nothing in the room that could protect her. She'd rather die than have him carry out his plan of forcefully making her submit, humiliating her, making her cower. There was some sadistic need in him to subdue women, especially strong ones.

The door opened, and Salazar stepped through. She caught a glimpse of a broad back before he closed the door. Even if she got through him, she'd have his thug to muscle through as well.

She heard the lock engage as he leaned nonchalantly against it. He was carrying a camera in his hand. "Shall we finish what we began, Dana?"

She kept the bed between them, knowing that finishing his ranting interview would only buy her a little time. Hopefully Bowie would get here in time before Hector...

She couldn't finish the thought.

She looked toward the door, and he chuckled. "There is no way he is going to get here in time, my lovely."

He pushed off the door and set the camera on the bed, and his eyes went over her from the top of her head, lingering over her breasts and traveling down the rest of her body. Her skin crawling, she tried with all her might not to react. He wanted the fear. The instinctive fear a woman had with a man whose intentions were not only impure, but violent.

She shivered when he smiled, his provocative look only

made her skin crawl. "Sure, Hector. Why don't we finish your interview?"

"Do you have your questions prepared?"

"I would only need a few minutes."

"Liar!" he shouted all of a sudden, a light in his eyes that told her he'd had no intention of finishing his rant. This was all about intimidating her. Fear rising up from the pit of her stomach, radiating to her extremities, she grabbed the camera off the bed. She threw it at him as she raced for the door. But there was no way out. It was as locked as it was before.

He grabbed her by the hair and slapped her hard across the face, the sting of the blow making her eyes water. She reeled away off balance, her shoulder slamming against the wall, pain traveling down her arm to her fingertips.

"It's time you realized that there is only one man on this planet who can satisfy you."

As she stood there trying to work around the pain, Salazar advanced on her.

～

As soon as the chopper set down, Ruckus said, "Punch a hole through that line. Whatever it takes."

Tank caught the bazooka Hollywood threw at him and shot off a rocket. The explosion rocked the compound, and men started firing back at them.

"Blow the gates."

Wicked ran up to the iron structure, set his charges. "Breach!" he yelled as he moved a safe distance away and hit the detonator.

The blast was deafening as all eight SEALs opened fire

on the men who came pouring out of the gate that was now hanging off its hinges.

Hollywood, manning the 50 cal, mowed down a whole group of them. The smoke cleared enough to see that there was the hole he'd ordered. They advanced, taking care of stragglers they encountered, fighting their way to her.

Hang on, babe. I'm coming for you.

DANA WAS DETERMINED that she would not go willingly into this violation. She was going to fight with everything she had. She punched and kicked as he reached out for her, but he pressed her hard against the wall and sealed his mouth to hers. She violently pulled away, revulsion washing through her with an icy sickness. He backhanded her, stunning her enough to try to kiss her again. Instead of succeeding, she viciously bit him. He cried out and punched her hard in the stomach, sending her to her knees.

"You are just putting off the inevitable. And I really don't mind if you fight." He reached down and grabbed her hair, yanking her to her feet. She tried to hit him, breathing hard, tears washing down her cheeks, fear racking her like claws sunk into her gut.

He threw her on the bed and then covered her with his body. Before she could recover, he had a knife at her throat. "I would feel very cheated if I couldn't have you the way I want you. You will stop fighting me and surrender, or I will kill you now."

"You think I don't know this is what you wanted, you sick bastard? You were going to kill me anyway. Me, Liam, James. We were never getting out of this alive."

"Of course, when I leaked the interview with me and you, the media would have eaten it up. There would be so much speculation about what had happened to you out here, I would have gotten play of my words for years. If you stop fighting me, I promise it will be quick and painless. If you don't..."

She could barely breathe, the threat of the razor-sharp knife against her neck ready to cut into her unprotected skin. "I have no choice," she whispered, the triumph in his eyes making her wish like hell that she had done more with her personal life, lived it fuller and to the max instead of letting her guilt dictate and keep her from going after her own happiness. She regretted it now because she couldn't comply. She couldn't surrender this to him because it was her body, her decision. This was *her* life.

She was ready for him to hurt her bad, but as soon as he removed the knife, she went for his eyes with her thumbs. He screamed as she dug deep, bucked him off, and shoved him with all her might.

He came up yelling, blinking and searching for her. She had no idea how to disarm a man with a knife. No idea how she was going to stop him from killing her now because the threat and the promise were in his eyes.

All she knew was she couldn't give in. Would never give in. There was only one man in her life that she wanted to touch her, one man she wanted to explore and get to know, one man who she freaking loved. Salazar couldn't take that from her.

She braced herself as he came at her, even as there was a commotion in the hallway. Explosions and gunfire told her that the SEALs were here. They were coming for her, but it wasn't going to be in time. Salazar would gut her before they could stop him.

Gunfire in the distance had only gotten closer. Something heavy hit the door. Salazar rushed at her, but then it slammed open by some explosive force. Bowie and Wicked came through. Bowie's gun discharged, and Salazar jerked. He dropped the knife, and Dana reached out, grabbed his thumb, and brought him to his knees. Then she kicked him square in the nuts.

Bleeding and crying out in agony, Salazar fell to the floor, writhing.

Bowie was there, drawing her against him, holding her so tightly in his arms. She looked up at him, and Wicked said, "LT. We've gotta go, or we're going to get boxed in."

"Your memory cards," he whispered.

"I'm not willing to risk all our lives on them. Let's get out of here. He's never going to tell me where they are."

Blue checked Salazar. "He's alive." He shouldered him onto his back and said, "Let's roll."

THEY FORMED A WALL AROUND HER, and they started to move through the house, pausing when they encountered men they had to subdue, Echo distracting, charging in at Tank's command. They made it to the front door, fighting their way out, the SEALs a force to be reckoned with. They streaked across the compound, two of them breaking off and helping to clear the way. Finally, they were at the chopper, and all of them climbed inside. Dana clutched Ruckus, her eyes bruised and sad. He hadn't been able to get her what she wanted, needed. It was nothing new. Even though he wanted to say that he cared about her more than what had happened physically between them, he couldn't seem to get his mind around it.

They headed for the coast and the USS *Annenberg*. This mission was done. Tank landed the chopper on the deck a few minutes later. Blue whisked Salazar off to the infirmary, and Major McRae walked up to them and said, "Ms. Sorenson?"

Dana nodded, still looking way too pale.

"Are you okay, ma'am? Do you need medical attention?"

She shook her head. Clutching Ruckus, she followed the major into the main part of the aircraft carrier and a small theatre-like conference room. He said, "Have a seat."

Ruckus and the SEALs all sat down. "Ma'am, this is just a short debrief. I'm sure you're aware the nature of this mission was black, and to have any of this information leaked to any media outlet would undermine our ability to carry out such missions. We do appreciate your assistance in the capture and detainment of Hector Salazar but ask for your silence in this matter once you are back stateside. Can we rely on your discretion?"

"Yes," she said, looking at Ruckus. "If it wasn't for Lieutenant Cooper and the rest of his team, I wouldn't have ever left that stronghold the first time and definitely not the second. I appreciate all your efforts, and you have my word that I will never talk about this mission to anyone at all. Also, let me commend Lieutenant Cooper and his team for their professionalism, attention to duty, and determination. I simply wouldn't be sitting here if it hadn't been for Lieutenant Cooper's quick thinking, quick action, and patience with me. I am and will always be eternally grateful."

Her words sank in and the pride he felt for his team washed through him mixed with the humor of her being so damn professional at the moment after all they had been through in the Gap.

"Thank you, ma'am. That is good to know about my men. This is a top-notch team."

She nodded. "What happens now?"

"You will be flown to Panama City. You are booked on a commercial flight back to San Diego. I am truly sorry about your inability to recover your memory cards and your interviews."

"Thank you. I'm so thankful my crew was rescued. Is there any word about them?"

"Yes, Liam Nelson has been released to his family and is back home. James Quinn has woken up from his coma and is doing well. He's out of the woods."

"That is such good news."

"I'll be sure to give you information about where he is, so that you can visit."

She rose and shook the major's hand, then she turned.

She met his eyes. They filed out and when they reached the deck, Blue was already back on the chopper, ready for their trip off the aircraft carrier. She nodded to him, and he saluted her. She hugged each one of the SEALs, petting Echo, thanking them, and Ruckus's throat got really tight. Finally, she turned to him as they headed to the waiting chopper. "Is this going to be goodbye?"

He looked away, working to maintain his composure. "Yes. I'm not the kind of man you need in your life."

"How do you know what I need?"

"I'm just not good at relationships." When she went to protest, he covered her mouth and stepped into her, wrapping his arms around her. When he broke the kiss, he murmured, "Do you want to know what destroyed my marriage?"

"Yes," she whispered.

"The distance. And I'm not just talking about being deployed. That took its toll. She wanted something deeper, and I couldn't give it to her."

"What did she want?"

"Children," he said, his voice subdued, strained. "I said no fucking way. I'm no poster boy for a great childhood, and the father I had was nothing but a bastard to me. How would I raise my own children? I failed her, and I'll fail you, Dana. It's best we just leave it for what it was. A fight for survival where we needed to lean on each other to get the job done. I am truly sorry about your memory cards. Now you can go back to what you were doing. Giving everything you have to a cause."

"Bowie, that's not fair."

"It's fair, and you know it." He cupped her face and smiled into her beautiful eyes. "Don't waste your life trying to atone for what you think is your sin against your mom. Don't let all this beauty, all that you are get wasted on being too damned selfless and noble. Find what you want and take it like a pirate. Somewhere along the way, don't forget about me. Okay? I'll keep that part inside me."

He turned and walked back toward the waiting helicopter.

"Bowie!" she screamed his name as if her heart was shattering. He turned as she ran across the deck into his arms. He wrapped her in a tight embrace. Kissing her like he would never stop. Then with one final, intimate look from the depths of her eyes, he turned, mounted the running board of the chopper, and disappeared inside.

He closed his eyes, filled up to the brim with everything that had happened, everything she'd said.

As he heard the hollow echo of the chopper's blades

revving for liftoff, he took one last look at her through the glass. He was in love with her. His heart ached to be the man she could depend on—it nearly took his breath. It surprised him after all this time, after all the hard lessons, that he could still be vulnerable. He should have been able to steel himself against it. He should have known enough to turn away from the very beginning. But Dana was the kind of woman who made it damned difficult not to want more, and more...and fucking more.

He had wanted her from the first. Desire he understood. It was simple, basic, elemental. But this...this was something he could never trust. Giving himself body and soul. He'd never done it. Wasn't sure he was ever capable of handing over his heart. He was vigilant, but somewhere in that jungle, he'd lost it. Sweetness and courage had outdone him.

"You going to look her up when you get to San Diego?" Kid asked.

"I don't have her address," he murmured.

"I have it. It was part of the background check we ran. Some guys on the team know it, too. If you don't make a move, I think some of them might steal her away."

His jaw flexed. "No, it's better this way."

"For who, LT? Life is too short to not go for the gold."

Echo raised his head, his brown eyes on Ruckus as if he, too, agreed with Kid. His ears pricked forward.

"How do you know that, Kid? You're still wet behind the ears."

"Maybe so, but I know something's there when I see it, and with all due respect, sir, I know a fool when I see one, too."

"Shut up, Kid."

"Yes, sir. Copy that."

He couldn't allow himself to be in love with Dana Sorenson. She deserved far better than him.

FROM THE DECK of the aircraft carrier, she was transported to the terminal, and she clutched her pack, her heart aching. She waited for her flight, staring out of the big glass windows and into the urban sprawl of Panama City.

The flight was uneventful. The soft conversations, the scents of people and civilization scattered around her seemed more foreign to her than the jungle had been. People stared at her just a little bit longer than usual, wondering at the bruises on her face and the gash on her forehead. Wondering what ill had befallen her. But those bruises and that gash had been to save Bowie, and she'd gladly wear them like a badge.

When she landed in San Diego, she took a cab home. She went up to her bedroom and stripped down to nothing, preoccupied with turbulent thoughts of Bowie and the time they had spent together, his refusal to take a chance on her. She'd wanted to tell him then that she loved him. Wanted him to know how much she was willing to sacrifice to be with him. It wouldn't be a conventional relationship with the jobs they had, but it would have been so damned meaningful. She released a soft sob, letting the tears flow. He had taught her that life was worth living, worth finding happiness in everything that she did. Finally, her suffering, her guilt could be released. There was no need for it. Bowie had been right. In his own realization about moms, he had discovered their capacity to love. She hoped he took his knowledge and went home, went home to finally heal his own heart.

She took a long, warm shower. Afterward, she wiped the condensation off the mirror over the sink and assessed her looks, seeing black and blue, an angry red slash, and a woman with troubled eyes and damp, dark hair combed loosely back.

There should have been some external sign of the changes made inside her during the last three weeks—the strength she had regained fighting for her new friends, the humility that remained after she had realized her own emotions had been holding her back, that she had finally forgiven herself for not being there for her mom, starting to let herself grieve as Bowie had held her while she cried for her loss, cried for the woman who had nurtured her, molded her character and in the end become her best friend. The loss she recognized, the love she embraced, and the peace of knowing that even now, her love could not be diminished.

That could be said of Bowie as well. God, how she loved that man, his fierceness, his vulnerabilities, his courage, and his strong and noble heart. He wore his trident proud, and the navy should feel damn lucky to have him in their ranks. They had chosen a lost, bruised, and battered seventeen-year-old boy who had matured and come into his own. His accomplishments were varied and something he was modest about because his humility was also a part of him, the other side of that coin of confidence that was as natural on him as breathing.

She left the bathroom, dressed in a pair of gray shorts and a white tank top. She settled on her comfortable bed and picked up her phone. Settling back against the pillows, her exhaustion completely took her over. With heavy lids, she pulled up the pictures she'd taken of him. Her favorite had been right before the jaguar had crossed their path and she'd said all those naughty things to him to crack his focus. He'd been standing there, looking like he owned the jungle. Protective, so freaking gorgeous, exuding all that sexual magnetism. Her heart constricted, and her throat tightened as her eyes closed and she drifted to sleep, her tears dropping onto her pillow, her heartbreak complete.

15

It was early evening, the smell of honeysuckle in the hills of his home as familiar as his name. Being home, which was a pretty big misnomer, was as easy as slipping on an old, worn pair of shoes.

But he wasn't here to come home or feel at home. He was here to visit his mom after twenty years of estrangement. Dana had convinced him that getting all this done was the best thing for him. That's why he was doing this but letting go of his anger was something he didn't think he could do.

Not a day had gone by that he didn't think about her. Not since dropping off Salazar in DC to be taken into custody. Ruckus still wanted to kill the bastard with his bare hands. But justice would be served, and rumor had it that old Hector wasn't going to ever get his freedom. Killing federal agents warranted the death penalty. They had a pretty tight case against him, and as expected, Panama was happy to get rid of him.

The place had changed quite a bit. When his dad had been alive, there was nothing but dirt in front. The lawn had often been left unmowed until Ruckus did it himself with an ancient hand mower.

There were flowers and bushes now in front, the lawn lush and green. The porch had been repaired, and there were two rockers with a table in between them. A pitcher of lemonade and...two glasses.

There was laughter, and the front screen door opened, and his mom came out, a man following. He wrapped his arms around her and kissed her deeply. Caught in shock, Ruckus stared. The man raised his head and peered out to the walk.

"Who is that?" Ruckus challenged, and with another shock, he realized that the man was Sam Walker, the local real estate broker.

His mother turned around and then froze. The look of pain and hope on her face made him take a step back, as if he couldn't handle rejection from her again. She had said never to come back.

"Bowie is that you, son?"

Her voice was hushed, as though if she said too much, he might disappear into thin air. Before he could take a step forward, she rushed off the porch and threw her arms around him. "Oh my, you are so tall." He could hear the tears clogging her voice.

Unable to deny himself this hope, he wrapped his arms around her and said, "Yes, Mom, it's me."

"Come into the light, and let me look at you." She pulled him to the porch, and Sam stepped back, beaming at him.

He offered his hand and Ruckus took it, the man's grip tight and welcoming. "It's a pleasure to meet you, although I knew you when you were just a kid."

"Yes, I remember you."

"Sam and I are married," she said, wrapping her arm around his waist.

Sam cleared his throat. "Yeah, last year. We started going together a year after your daddy passed."

"You remarried?"

"Yes. I'm assuming you got the email about your father's death. He wasn't much of a man, but I thought you should know."

"I don't give a damn about him," Ruckus said, the anger that often accompanied those words gone.

"Why are you here, son?"

"I'll go make the salad, Beth, and start the steaks grilling. Will you be joining us?"

"Throw one on for him, honey. Let us have a few moments to talk."

Sam nodded and disappeared into the house, and his mom sat down in one of the rockers. "Have a seat. Let's get this started."

"I'm here to ask you why you threw me out? Why you abandoned me? All I wanted to do was protect you."

She took a deep breath. "That's all I wanted for you, my boy. When you knocked him out, and I saw how powerful you had grown, I knew that your father would most likely kill you or you'd kill him. I didn't want my only child, my boy, to have to do something drastic like that. I ran you off because I knew you had the navy, and they would be the right choice for you. I was so proud when you graduated from the SEALs."

"Wait, you were there?" His lungs felt compressed, his heart turning over.

"Yes, I was there. Your father wouldn't have seen kindly to it, so when the invitation came from the navy, I hid it, made up a story about going to see my sister, and went off to

Coronado. I'm so happy that I was there to see you come into your own. Are you still serving?"

"Yes. I plan to serve until I retire. I'm a lieutenant now."

She beamed. "I was so hoping that one day you would come home so we could clear the air. I have been so happy with Sam. He is so good to me, and we have a great life. But it would be so much better if you were in it."

He bowed his head, and she came off the rocker and knelt, pulling him to her. It had been years since he let himself think about this moment. His mom holding him to her. His heart feeling as if it was going to break under the pain. He had to let go of the anger that was inside him. He had to let go and forgive, move on, allow her back into his life. Silent tears rolled down his face, and he held her just as tightly.

"I'm sorry, Bowie. I know this has been so hard on you. But it's over now and both of us can forgive. Sam was the one who told me to write you that email, and if it brought you to me, I will be so grateful."

"It was more than the email, Mom. I met this amazing woman."

He told her about Dana, and as he spoke, he realized that he'd been wrong. He was husband material, friend material, son material. He had always been. It had taken Dana and her compassionate heart to listen to him, see what he was missing, and encourage him to reconcile.

"When you can, you bring her around. I need to meet her. Sam has two grown children and three grandchildren. I so want you to get to know them as well."

It was then he realized that he needed Dana in his life. He needed his mom and her new family in his life. It was fuller and richer now because of Dana. He loved her. His gut clenched. He'd never said it first. It was his rule.

He wasn't sure if she'd done what she needed to for her own closure. But for the first time since he'd said goodbye to her on the deck of the USS *Annenberg*, he was sure that he was going to damn well find out.

Just as he finished the delicious meal with his mom and Sam, his cell chimed. "Mom, they're calling me in. I've got to go."

On the porch, she hugged him hard. "Stay safe, and let me know when you return home. When we can plan a get together."

He hugged her hard and shook Sam's hand. "Thank you for taking care of my mom."

"She's the best," Sam said.

Ruckus was sorry that he'd wasted so many years not knowing his mom, but he pushed that aside. There was no longer any room in his life for bitterness, and his only regret was not taking what Dana had been offering.

By the time he got back to Coronado, he discovered he and the team were going back aboard the USS *Annenberg* and back into the Darién Gap. Hector Salazar had given up Angel Nunez, his second-in-command. He'd been the one to plan and carry out the murders. He was now their HVT package.

But when they inserted and made their way to the compound, there was no one to be found. The place had been abandoned, and Nunez was in the wind.

"What now, LT?" Cowboy asked.

Ruckus said, "I'd like to turn this place upside down and see if we can locate Dana's memory cards."

"Copy that," he said with a grin. "Let's go, ladies."

They worked from the top of the place to the bottom, but no cards. "Where would that bastard hide them?"

"I think I know," Kid said. He ran back upstairs and

came back with several cameras, and sure enough, inside were the cards, hiding in plain sight.

Once they were in the chopper, Kid nudged him and said, "Now you'll have to go see her, LT. I bet she's going to be happy to see you."

                      ~

A WEEK after she got back to San Diego, she sat in Liam's living room visiting with him and his wife Selma. She'd spent the first few days visiting with Liam, and he looked tired and haunted, admitting to her that he was seeing someone to help with the nightmares that plagued him.

"I'm so happy that you're safe, Dana. I never trusted Salazar for one moment after I saw the way he was looking at you. We're all so lucky to be alive."

"We are," she said, accepting the cup of coffee from his wife. Their three-year-old daughter Jennifer was playing with blocks near the sliding glass door.

Selma said, "I was so worried about him. I hope you don't have any plans for any more trips into dangerous places because Liam and I discussed it. And, well, he's going to take a job with a local news desk here in San Diego as one of their producers. I hope you understand. I want him home, and after coming so close to losing him—" Her voice broke. "I can't handle him going off any more."

"Would you be willing to edit stuff for me, Liam?"

He took his wife's hand, and Selma gave him a smile and a nod.

"Of course, but my trekking days are over. I want to be home at night for Selma and a dad to Jenny. I've already missed so much of her growing up already."

"I totally understand."

At the end of their visit, he hugged her hard.

"You are the frigging best I've ever worked with across the globe, my girl. Please take care of yourself and say hi to James when you see him. Let him know that we'll be up there tomorrow for a visit."

"I will." She left Liam's pretty neighborhood and drove to the hospital. James had been admitted after the navy had flown him home. When she entered his room, carrying the flowers she'd purchased, he was sitting up in bed. He beamed at her when she walked in. The room was filled with balloons, cards, more flowers, some plants, and even a teddy bear.

"Oh, my God," she said, tears in her voice. "It's so good to see you." He hugged her hard, holding her tightly. Gratitude toward not just the navy, but for the role Bowie and his team had played, filled her. She kissed his cheek. "How are you?"

"I'm mending. I'm still having some headaches, but the docs tell me that's normal. I'll be out of here in a week."

"Do you have somewhere you can stay?"

"Yeah, Liam's offered me his spare room, and his wife Selma has graciously offered to nurse me. She used to be an R.N. before she quit her job after Jenny was born."

"That's good to know. Then I can visit you both."

"I'm glad you're home in one piece," he murmured. "He didn't...hurt you, did he?"

Sweet, protective James. He'd been injured because he was fighting to help her. Worried about her.

"No, he never got the chance. I was protected and rescued by eight very large, very in charge Navy SEALs."

He nodded, and she took his hand. "All that matters now is for you to get well."

Deep down inside, she missed Bowie so much. Even an hour without him had felt so empty. She had wanted him in her life, but he hadn't been able to see himself there. Maybe she was in love with him, but maybe he didn't feel the same way about her. She spent an hour with James, and by then, it was late afternoon. She figured it was time to go see her dad, Bowie heavy on her mind. She wanted to get closure. As she pulled into his driveway and parked next to his sedan, her cell phone rang. She answered.

"Hi, Dana. It's Jeff. I know we agreed that you needed time to yourself after what happened to you, but I was wondering if it would be okay for me to come by tonight." Her conscience was clear, and she had clarity for the first time in a long time. She was sorry that she had to hurt his feelings.

She took a deep breath. "Yes, that's fine."

She got out of her car and heard the saw going. Her father had a workshop behind the house and made furniture now that he'd retired from nursing. It also kept him busy, so he wouldn't think about the loss of his wife.

As she went around the back of the house, her cell rang again. She answered, thinking it was Jeff again.

"Did you forget something?"

"Hello," the unfamiliar voice said.

"Oh, I'm sorry. I thought you were someone else."

"Is this Dana Sorenson?"

"Yes, it is. How can I help you?"

"This is Sara Campbell from KASD here in San Diego. I have an offer for you."

"An offer?"

"Yes. I'm a friend of Liam Nelson; he's done some work for me. He mentioned your trip to the Darién Gap, and I'm thoroughly intrigued by your story. I've been following your career ever since he mentioned you. We have an opening on our international desk, and I'd love for you to come work for me. I know this grounds you a bit, but I can promise you the excitement of a war correspondent and a freelancer doing stories across the globe. I like what you've come up with so far. I'm open to anything you might like to do—documentaries, history pieces, investigative, and something I know is close to your heart, the human condition."

Dana wasn't sure what to say. Being grounded in San Diego, the possibility of being in one place long enough to make a life with someone, was appealing to her.

"I know this is a lot to process," she said. "Take some time and let me know when you're ready. Say next week? We could have lunch and discuss it."

"Yes. Thank you so much for calling."

Suddenly unable to face her dad right now, she paced the narrow flag walk, the agitation splintering into a dozen different reactions. Grateful. She was grateful to be recognized for her accomplishments. She was terrified—the thought of letting go of her vagabond life and the work she thought her mom wanted her to do making her jittery. Then there was the anger. Anger at Bowie over his refusal to recognize how much he truly had to offer her. If she could be sure about one thing, he was in love with her. She was certain of it. But it was so hard to go against all that had piled up against him over the years. She closed her eyes, feeling his loss keenly. She could only hope he would find his way out. That man was so damn brave in so many ways, but what made her melt, made her want more of him, was the vulnerability he let her see. That had done her in.

She went to the workshop door, and when her dad saw her, he smiled broadly, flipped off the saw, and removed his safety goggles. Rushing behind the work bench, he grabbed her up in a strong embrace and held her tightly for several minutes. Her throat constricted.

"My baby is back. I was so worried about you, sweetheart."

"I know, and I'm sorry you had to go through that."

"Come in the house. Have you had lunch?" he said over his shoulder as she followed him.

"No. I've been to see Liam and James."

"Oh, yes. How are they doing?"

"Fine. Liam isn't going to be doing anymore overseas projects. James is probably going to retire."

He went to the fridge and pulled out ham and some potato salad. In her family, he was the cook and the manager. Her mother had been brilliant, but she relied on her dad for the everyday necessities to be done. It made him a strong, independent guy who didn't need his daughter hovering around him.

He made them both a sandwich and dished up a heaping spoonful of potato salad and some corn on the cob. Dana loved it cold. He brought the plates to the patio table and then went back for glasses of iced tea.

The sandwich was delicious, and she polished off half, not realizing how hungry she'd been. "Did you ever resent that Mom didn't help you around the house?"

"Lord, no. She had her journals and articles to write. Always busy. I loved taking care of her. I was definitely the domestic one."

"Both of you were so...selfless, caring, giving. I tried to be like you both."

He studied her, her pensive tone coming across loud and clear. "What is it, sweetie?"

"I-I had a hard, so very hard time not being there when she died. I promised."

He rose immediately at the sound of the pain in her voice. "Oh, honey. I know. I was devastated, too. But she knew we loved her, and she went so fast. I'm sure she didn't suffer at all."

"That's just the thing. All this time I haven't allowed myself to mourn her, Dad." Tears streamed down her face and she wiped at her cheeks. "I have sacrificed so much of my life trying to be like you both."

"We didn't expect that, Dana. We were happy when you were happy doing what you wanted." He hugged her close, and she pressed her face against his chest, her tears soaking into his cotton shirt. He smelled so good, so Dad to her. "I thought it was what you wanted. Maybe you should take some time. Figure out what you want to do with your life." She nodded, her throat tight. "Your mother was very proud of you, Dana. Never forget that, ever."

"I love you, Dad."

"I love you, too, honey." They stood that way for a while as she remembered her mother, and she was sure that her dad was also thinking about her. She took solace in his arms, missing her mom, missing Bowie, and not sure exactly what she was going to do with her life. But the station offer made her feel good, grounded her like she'd wanted to be grounded. She told her dad, and his enthusiasm fueled her own. Maybe it was time she followed her own heart.

When she got home, she showered and changed, her mind on Jeff. She was dreading this meeting with him and had been dreading it from the moment she'd first kissed Bowie's sexy mouth. The memory of the wild sex they had against the tree overwhelmed her senses, even as the doorbell rang.

She opened the door, and Jeff was standing there, a bottle of wine in his hands. He really was quite a nice man, which only made her guilt much worse. Willing away the queasy feeling, her anxiety skyrocketed as he leaned in and gave her a quick kiss. Something Bowie would never have done. He would have been very thorough.

She had to stop thinking about him. He was out of her life.

"Come in. Thanks for the wine."

He entered, his hair styled, his suit pristine, and all she could think about was Bowie's unruly hair, the delicious stubble on his face, the way she'd touched him when she'd shaved him for the resort. How he'd looked at her the last few seconds before he'd walked away.

Her nerves jangling, she went into the living room and said, "Why don't you have a seat, and I'll get us some of this wine? Where did you want to go for dinner?"

"Anywhere is fine," he said. "You choose."

Nothing really appealed to her, but she figured after they had their talk, Jeff wouldn't have an appetite for dinner. The queasiness was back. She wasn't exactly looking forward to it either.

Once she returned from the kitchen, she handed him a glass and took a sip. He patted the sofa. "Why don't you sit down?"

"All right," she said, and settled on the cushion next to him.

"Dana, I've been thinking for some time—"

"I can't marry you," she blurted out. She rose and paced. He had this surprised look on his face, and she rushed on. "Something happened when I was in the Darién Gap, something that would never have happened if I was in love with you, committed to you."

He leaned back against the sofa, taking a sip of his wine. "What happened?"

"I can't go into too much detail... I met someone. He

helped me out several times, but that isn't the reason I love him."

"It isn't?" he asked, his voice neutral, and she had to wonder if he was hiding his disappointment.

"No, he's so compassionate, a good listener—"

"You'd have to be with you, Dana."

She nodded, then stopped and gave him a narrow look. "What is that supposed to mean?"

"You know very well what it means," he said with amusement. "Come on and sit down."

"You're disappointed in me, aren't you," she said, feeling so awful.

He started to laugh, and she set down her wine glass, her hands going to her hips. "What's so funny? Here you are ready to ask me to marry you—"

"I wasn't going to ask you to marry me."

She stared at him for a minute. "No?"

"Nope." He stood and steered her to the sofa. "Will you please sit?"

"I need a drink," she whispered, folding down. "You weren't going to ask me?"

He shook his head. "No, I was going to tell you that we should break up, see other people. I have a wonderful girl in mind, but we've been there for each other, you for my dad and me for your mom. I think we knew that it wasn't working. That's why we stopped seeing so much of each other. I still want to be friends with you, Dana, but that's all."

"That's all? Just friends?" She closed her eyes and sighed. "I'm so relieved."

When she didn't say anything more, he said, "Are you okay?"

She smiled and hugged him. "Yeah, I think I am. You?"

"Very much so."

She sat back.

"How about we go to dinner for old times' sake, and I'll tell you about Vanessa."

"Is this the girl?"

"Yes. She works one office over from me, and I think she's great." He hesitated, then looked pained. "Is this too soon?"

"No. Vanessa?" she prompted. They rose, and he continued to catalog the woman's qualities all the way to the door.

Before they could leave, the bell rang. "Are you expecting someone?"

She pulled open the door, and he was standing there. Lieutenant Bowie "Ruckus" Cooper was dressed in a pair of sinfully tight jeans, a plain blue shirt that had Navy across it in white, and a black leather jacket. He had a light stubble on his face, and his hair was windblown.

For a moment, she couldn't speak. Bowie eyed Jeff in his very scary SEAL way, and for a moment, she worried about Jeff's welfare.

"Bowie?"

"Yeah, I need to talk to you, cupcake. Is this a bad time?"

"Cupcake?" Jeff asked with a smirk. "She actually let you get away with calling her that?"

"Who's the suit?" he asked.

"Jeffrey Snyder, this is Lieutenant Cooper. Navy SEAL."

"The boyfriend," Bowie growled.

"Ah, I think that's my cue to skedaddle. Good luck, Lieutenant. You're going to need it." He bussed her cheek and squeezed out the door.

"Are you going to invite me in or keep me very inhospitably here on your porch?"

"No, of course not. Come in. Geez, you haven't changed a bit."

He walked past her, the whiff of him almost buckling her knees. He filled up her house and her heart, but she couldn't let herself hope.

"Why are you here?"

He looked around. "This is real nice. It's exactly the way I thought it would be. You look good, babe."

"So do you."

He shifted and said, "So is that guy out of your life or are you marrying him?"

"What's it to you? You said you weren't interested."

"Damn, woman. That's not what I said. I thought you deserved better."

She narrowed her eyes. "Don't tell me I'm a bad judge of character. I know what I want!"

"Is that so?"

"Yes."

"Every damn conversation with you has to be an argument."

"You're the one shouting."

He took two strides to her and pulled her against him. "Well, at least I know one way to win an argument with you."

Before she could so much as utter a comeback or realize his intent, he captured her mouth with his. Her lips parted as she sucked in a quick, startled breath, and he shoved his fingers into her hair and held her head in his hands, rendering her immobile as he delivered a demanding, tongue-tangling kiss she couldn't escape. Knowing how tough and obstinate she was, he wasn't at all gentle with her.

He shifted closer and poured everything into the hot, ruthless kiss—aggression, dominance, and a desperate need. Fire pooled in her belly and lower, her pique mingling with an undeniable need for him to possess her in every way imaginable. She didn't resist him as he continued to consume her mouth the same way she wanted to ravish his body with her lips, teeth, and tongue, and the craving for him grew stronger, a ravenous heat and hunger she had only experienced with him.

When he broke the kiss, she looked up at him. "Why are you here?"

He took a breath and stepped back from her. Narrowing his eyes, he said, "I have something for you."

He reached into the pocket of those sexy jeans and pulled out a plastic bag.

She looked at the bundle in his hand, then up at him, her vision blurring. Something inside her let go. All of it, her guilt, her need to constantly put herself out there for some test she didn't need to take. When that dam let go, the grief for her mom simply came flooding out. She thought she'd let herself go when she'd first come home, but that had only been the tip of the iceberg. Her sorrow at losing Bowie was all wrapped up in it, keeping her from fully feeling. The numbing effects from the three weeks in the Darién Gap and the safety of home all made her knees weak.

She covered her face as the huge dam inside her burst, crashing, cascading emotions rolling out like flood waters. She missed her mom; it hurt so much, the sick guilt gone, washed away by the rending. She wanted to change everything, and she was so in love with this man, there was no going back, no letting go, nowhere to turn but his arms.

And he was there as fresh tears spilled down her cheeks, and her voice was a tortured whisper. "Bowie..."

A deep racking sob broke from her when he caught her

against him in a crushing embrace. Bowie's expression twisted into a grimace as he roughly gathered her close, his hold fierce.

A shudder coursed through him, his voice hoarse and shaking as he choked out, "Dana."

Driven by need and love, Dana twisted her head free from his hold, searching for his mouth, and a low, satisfied sound tore from him as the searing contact unleashed a frantic hunger. He groaned again, his embrace becoming almost brutal as her breath caught on a ragged sob, and he ground his mouth against hers, his control completely shattered. Fueled by days of separation, their reunion was nothing short of desperate, left no room for conscious thought, propelling them into a consuming passion. The only thing Dana knew was the granite hardness of his body locked against hers and the crushing strength of his arms.

Like a drowning man battling for breath, Bowie roughly grasped her head and tore his mouth away, his face contorted as he fought to haul air into his lungs. His chest heaved when he finally looked at her, his eyes so blue and filled with the mirror of her own.

He swallowed hard as he cupped the back of her head. His eyes were mesmerizing as he caressed her scalp, then slowly, so slowly, he lowered his head, his touch immeasurably tender as he brushed his mouth against hers.

That soft, lingering kiss drove the strength out of her, enervating her with a thick, pulsating weakness, and her eyes drifted shut as she swayed against him, hypnotized by the magic of his touch. His hand cupped her temple as he lightly moved his mouth back and forth across hers, slowly savoring her warmth, trying to soothe her raw emotions. He inhaled jaggedly as he shuddered again, his obvious struggle for control igniting a wild clamor that demanded more. With a soft moan, she caught the back of his head, the gentleness turning into a fierce and escalating need as the kiss deepened and turned hot and searching.

He pulled away just enough to lock gazes with her.

"I have a great headboard that has some really stellar handholds."

His eyes darkened, and his hand tightened in her hair. He closed his eyes and whispered, "You asking me to fuck you so good?"

"Just as long and as hard as your eyes are telling me you want to."

He snagged her hand and set it against the bulge in his pants. "No way a man can hide what he wants."

She molded her hand over him, and he caught his breath. She slid her hands beneath the leather jacket and pushed it off his shoulders and dropped it on the couch. Excitement erupted in her as she raked her hands through his silky hair, then across his shoulders. The muscles in his back tensed as he watched her, his eyes kindling, his body tightening against the sensations she aroused in him. His jaw flexed, and his nostrils flared as she slowly smoothed her hands back up his arms.

His eyes heated, then drifted shut as he breathed her name in a hoarse whisper. She touched his mouth with her trembling fingers, then, blinking back tears, eased away from him. He caught her head, his eyes smoldering as he tried to draw her to him.

But she resisted, pressing her fingers against his lips. "Don't, Bowie," she whispered brokenly. "If you touch me again, I won't be able to stop." She managed an unsteady smile as she caressed his cheek. "I want a bed. I want you so many ways in my bed."

He clenched his teeth, his whole body rigid. Then,

sucking in a deep breath, he gave her one hard kiss and simply bent his knees and shifted her into his arms.

"Where's the bedroom?" he growled.

"Upstairs, turn left, second door. You think you can handle finding it?"

"I'd find it in the dark, blind, cupcake."

He made his way, carrying her so easily as if she weighed nothing, his strong arms so hard and solid beneath her body.

He entered her room, and at the bedside, let her slide down his body. He dropped the plastic bundle on the bedside table, the soft glow from the lamp illuminating his strong, gorgeous features.

She stared up at him, a charge building between them as their gazes locked. She never took her eyes off his face as she slipped her hands across his shoulders and down his arm, stripping his shirt from him. A pulsating warmth spread through her body as she stared into his eyes, her hands trembling as she let them slip down his hard abdomen to his waist, where she undid the buckle of his belt, then slowly pulled his zipper down. He remained motionless, and she smoothed her hands down his hips, peeling the fabric away. But the minute she touched his swollen flesh, he reacted, and with a low, ragged groan, he pulled her roughly into his arms, their hips flushing together with a desperate surge.

He locked one arm around her buttocks, the other hand buried in her hair as he sought her lips, driving her into a mindless ecstasy as he moved against her, his body hard and thrusting, his mouth plundering hers. A fever of desire scorched through her, and Dana lost touch with reality as she responded to him.

Bowie rasped out her name as he roughly stripped her

garments from her, his need finally raging out of control. Then he crushed her against him and dragged her down to the bed, their bodies fusing together from shoulder to thigh. She didn't want him struggling to regain control or gentleness; she fed their desperation and the urgency, crying out her need as she grabbed onto the headboard, her hips rising to meet his powerful thrusts.

There was no going back or recovering from this. That chance was gone. He drove into her again and again, his body moving powerfully against hers, their desire breaking around them, carrying them away in the ultimate rush. The release was explosive, welding them together in a white-hot eruption.

16

When he woke up, light held at bay by her blinds and heavy curtains, he knew from his internal watch it was early morning. When he glanced at her bedside clock and saw the time, he realized that his military training had ingrained rising early into his very cells.

His eyes settled on the woman sleeping next to him. This was foreign to him, feeling like he wanted to do her again and never leave her side. In the past, he'd just gotten up, dressed, and left. No ties, no binds, no attachments.

Then she exploded into his life in terry cloth and attitude. Now, he knew he didn't want to leave here without some kind of a commitment. His heart sank when he realized that he couldn't expect her to deal with his life as a SEAL. Mary Jo hadn't, couldn't. Of course, he hadn't really helped there. He'd destroyed their marriage and thrown her love for him back in her face.

He took a breath, remembering his mom's words. That was all in the past. All of it. He'd let it go. Dana, she was his future if she would have him. He trembled at the power she had over him, over the situation, but his alpha bullshit wasn't going to help him here. With her. She'd walk all over his macho crap and then laugh in his face.

Damn but he loved that about her.

He reached out and pushed the covers off her, his breath catching at how beautiful she was. His heart ached, and his throat tightened. He would bawl like a baby if she was going to marry that guy who walked out of here last night.

She opened those honey brown eyes and they went over his face. She smiled softly. "Thank you for bringing back my memory cards." She shifted and wrapped her arms around his neck, an intimate warmth lighting up her eyes as her smile faded slightly. He kissed her, her mouth soft and warm.

She nuzzled his neck, sighing.

"You went through a lot for them. We had an opportunity to go back. I can't go into the details, but I looked for them for you."

"You are so wonderful." She moved deeper into his embrace, and he cradled her against his shoulder. Resting her head on his chest, she snuggled against him, and he knew he'd never get tired of this.

"Are you going to marry that guy?"

She lifted her head and stared at him, bemused and looking so sexy and mussed up. She frowned in an indulgent way. "What kind of person do you think I am? I wouldn't be lying here on your gloriously naked, hard, and gorgeous body if I had pledged to marry someone last night!"

He rubbed his temple, realizing that he was a complete idiot. Of course she wasn't. It was just his own fears. He wanted her to say it out loud.

"Right. Look, I'm an idiot, and I just woke up."

"Sure," she said, brushing over his lips. "You can't fool

me with that. You wake up as intense and completely ready for action as you are when you're awake."

He buried his face in her neck and breathed out a heavy, ragged sigh. "I just wanted to hear you say it."

She leaned back and cupped his face. "Oh, you did, did you?" She grinned at him, and his heart turned over. God, he wished she would just say it first.

"Did you just come back to return my memory cards?"

"No," he said. He rubbed at his stubble, his gut clenching. "I owe you dinner."

She huffed a breath and went to throw back the covers, but he grabbed her wrist and jerked her onto his chest. "Dammit! All right! I came back for you."

She stared at him for a second, then asked in a husky voice, "What's all the shouting about? You don't need to hide it from me."

He took a breath, soothed by her answer.

"For as long as you're here, you're staying with me. Where are your things?"

"You know I live in San Diego."

"I know you do. Where are your things?"

"In the car."

"Go get them. We've got a morning run, then we'll figure out what we want to do after that." Then she kissed him hard, slipped out of bed and into the bathroom. All he saw was the length of her dark hair swinging and that shapely backside.

He sighed, the moment gone. He'd wanted to tell her so badly, but he wanted to know at the same time. Since he didn't, he did as she'd asked and went for his duffel.

Time passed over the course of the next week. She got her crew on board, getting prepared to edit her footage and put together her story. He hung out at her house, watching her work, enjoying her when she wasn't.

He was sound asleep when a slap to his butt woke him up. "Get up. Let's go!" she said, and before he knew what was happening, she was out of bed. Startled, he watched that ball of energy grab up clothes, some flying toward him, others covering those delectable curves.

"Hey, babe. I had other plans. I wanted to compound on those orgasms last night."

She took a hard, quick breath. "I was faking." She giggled at his expression, then was gone. He thrust back the covers and barely got his running clothes and his shoes on before she was going out the door.

She rushed ahead of him, and he felt like he was laboring to catch his breath.

"Hold up, woman."

"Come on, slowpoke," she urged.

"Geez, what have you been doing since I've been gone? Running marathons?" he groused.

"Yes. I've got to keep up with you. I've been lifting weights, too. Wanna arm wrestle?"

He chuckled and stopped running. The sky was blue, and his heart was so damn full. "Dana, wait. You're tiring me out."

"That's my plan. Wear you out, wear you down. Like Chinese water torture." She stopped and turned toward him, then came running back.

"Come on, Grandpa, you can do it without your walker."

He grabbed her arm and drew her around, his face serious.

She sobered, the smile disappearing. Shit was about to get real.

"You're going to make me say it first. Aren't you?"

She closed her eyes briefly and then opened them, wetting her tantalizing lips. "Yes, I am."

"Out here in the park, under the heavenly blue sky, me all sweaty, hanging by a thread, scared as hell."

"Then you better say it before you waste away. I wouldn't like that."

He took a breath, his heart beating hard. He never said it first. It was one of the rules that he always played by, but Dana had discovered that if something wasn't working, she must be playing by the rules. They were meant to be broken, and he'd done his fair share of it to get the job done. She was definitely the woman for him. He stepped closer to her, framed her face in his hands, staring deeply into her eyes.

"I love you," he said, his tone low and rough. "I love the strong, independent woman you are. Arguing with you is the highlight of my day. I love the way you laugh, the way you make me laugh, your loopy sense of humor." His voice went even more ragged and soft. "I love making love to you."

She grasped his wrists, and her fingers tightened around them.

"But I especially love the way you make me feel alive when I thought I was just this scarred, bitter warrior. I can't live without that, Dana. I loved you every waking moment since I realized I loved you. So, there, I said it first. You made this alpha man heel."

She just stood there looking up at him, and his heart squeezed really hard, his fear running like ice through him. What if she didn't say it back?

"*Goddamn,* woman. Say something."

"I'm pretty attached to you, too."

For a minute he stood there, then she giggled. He growled and dragged her against him. "Dana, for the love of God and country."

She threw herself at him, wrapped her arms around his neck and shouted, "I love you, Bowie Cooper. My Ruckus, the man who saved me, the man I want for the rest of my life. I really love the way you make me feel. You gave me closure when I was so lost. You helped me find my mom again, and for that I'll be forever grateful to you." She kissed him. "You'll need all your SEAL skills to handle me."

"Don't I know it." When she went to kiss him again, he pulled back. "Wait. I know that being with me is going to take a toll. Deployments are hard on family members. But the SEALs, Dana, they are my family. I don't know—"

She covered his mouth and gazed up at him with so much love sparkling in her eyes, he'd been a fool to miss it. "I would never ask you to give up what you love. Will it be hard? Yes, it will, but I would rather be with you like this than live without you. I simply can't do that."

"I love you so much, Dana. I've been waiting my whole life for a woman like you."

"Then why did it take you so long to come back to me?"

"I was scared I wouldn't be the man you needed, wanted. I was afraid to hear you tell me those words."

"You really are a such a macho idiot, but you made me see that I was taking my objectivity as a reporter a step further and numbing everything, not just my professional life, but my personal life, too."

"I was an idiot until I went home, found my mom and she told me why she turned me out." He explained everything to her and her eyes went all soft and tender as he opened up. He felt safe with her, even with the dark stuff that had been trapped inside. She would never betray him.

She gave him such a tender look. "You weren't an idiot about that at all. Not at all." She hugged him hard, then said,

"Let's run really fast back home so I can show you how much I love you."

WHEN THEY GOT THERE, Ruckus groaned long and loud when he saw the SUV and the 4x4 sitting outside Dana's house. Dana was still basking in the glow of having this man show her his vulnerable side. She'd already seen the brave. Now she would cherish both so very much.

Seven very large figures were milling around. Cowboy in his distinctive black hat; Blue, aviator sunglasses glinting in the sun; Kid Chaos in a gray hoodie, looking tough and petulant; Tank, big, intimidating, with the most devastating dark eyes; Wicked looking tall, dark, and handsomely dangerous; Hollywood making her neighbors stop and stare; and last, but not least, Scarecrow with his smooth Southern accent and lean, mean body.

"Looks like we're outnumbered."

"This is a major goat fuck if I ever saw one," he said.

Dana laughed out loud when all those gorgeous, muscled hunks turned in their direction. "Love you, love your team?"

"Yeah, something like that. Although, I don't love them so much right now."

When she approached, she got high fives and devastating grins. She unlocked the door and all of them piled inside. She had a decent sized house, but these eight men filled it up to bursting as if there wasn't enough oxygen or square footage in the room.

"Why are you guys here?" Bowie asked.

"Man," Kid said. "You've been AWOL from the gym too

long, my friend, and the basketball court. We need you to even out the teams."

"Yeah, we missed you barking orders at us, LT," Blue said with a whine. "Kid cries himself to sleep every night. He misses your bedtime stories."

Kid hit Blue in the arm. "Shut up," he said, wiping away a mock tear. "Don't play on a man's pain."

Bowie set his hands on his hips. "So what are you going to do? Kidnap me?"

Kid walked up and bent at the knees, and before Dana could take another breath, he lifted Bowie into a fireman's carry. "See you in a bit, Dana. Breakfast would be nice." Kid grinned. "We'll be ravenous when we get back."

"You plan on bringing him back, then?" She grinned wide.

"Sure. You a good cook?"

"She is," Bowie said wryly from behind Kid's back.

Blue held the door, and Cowboy shook his head. "Sorry about this, ma'am, but it's SEAL business."

"I got your six. I'll make steak and eggs."

All of them cheered, many of them grinning, and Dana smiled. She may have fallen in love with Lieutenant Bowie "Ruckus" Cooper, but he came with this package deal, seven gorgeous alpha males with enough testosterone to light up every woman in the city, long deployments, and intense danger. She wasn't new to that last part, being a correspondent, but she and that big, wonderful man would make it work no matter what. And if it didn't work, well, then they'd break the rules and make new ones.

EPILOGUE

Dana put the finishing touches on her copy and queued up her footage. Bowie had been deployed for so long, she'd lost track of the time. In the interim, she ended up going to DC and finishing her interview with Hector Salazar, only she'd put her own spin on the finished product. Her new boss loved the angle. It hadn't taken them long to bond and become good friends. The picture of Bowie she'd taken in the jungle sat on her desk. She stared at it, picking it up, missing him. Their last skype session was too long ago.

Sara walked into the office, looking as put together as usual. The woman knew how to wear anything designer and wear it to the max, her long blond hair clipped at the nape of her neck. Dana guessed she was somewhere in her mid-thirties. She knew that body had been developed over Pilates, good nutrition, and yoga.

"How long has it been?" Sara asked.

"Too long," Dana replied and set the photo down.

"When was the last time you heard from him?"

Dana sighed. "Just a week, but I miss his physical presence."

"From that picture, I assume it's pretty damn potent. He is one gorgeous hunk of man." She sat down. "How do you handle that?"

Dana folded her arms over her chest and leaned back in her chair. "I know he's coming home to me." She leaned forward and woke her computer. "I wanted to—"

"Uh, Dana?" Sara's gaze sharpened then she smiled.

"What?" Dana said, focusing on Sara's joyful grin.

"I think your wait is over." She nudged her chin toward the outer office.

"What...?" Dana swiveled in her chair. Her breath caught like it always did, like it always would.

He was walking through the newsroom, female heads turning, eyes full of appreciation and envy. He was still in uniform, straight off the plane, it seemed. The only thing missing was that wicked rifle and the pack he carried. He looked way too sexy, and her whole body heated. They watched his progress, big, beautiful, and fresh from battle.

Their eyes met across the space, and she smiled. He smiled back. The kind of smile that told her handholds were in her not-too-distant future.

"I assume you're taking the rest of the day off."

Dana didn't even look at her boss. "Yeah," she said and got up, leaving everything running. Sara would take care of it for her.

When she reached him, she said softly, "Hello, sailor. Wanna have a good time?"

He grinned. "With a cupcake?"

"Sure. Why not?"

"You're not the argumentative type, are you? I can't stand it when a woman doesn't know her place."

"What kind of question is that to ask a grown woman?" She poked him in the chest. "You *caveman*."

He chuckled, his eyes telling her that's exactly the answer he was looking for. He kissed her in front of everyone. She melted against him while the office breathed a collective sigh and went back to work.

"Let's go home," he whispered.

~

EARLY EVENING LIGHT filtered in the windows as he shifted on the bed, a kind of stillness settling in that could only be found in deep contentment.

Dana lay on her stomach, sheets twisted around them both. Just barely awake and fuzzy from sleep and a night of very good loving. He was determined they weren't moving from this spot for days...weeks.

"How did it go?"

"You know I work with knuckleheads, right?"

"Yes," she breathed, wrapping her arm around him. "Everyone is safe?"

Her voice was hushed, and he understood that it wasn't only him she worried about. "Kid fell down an embankment right into a camp of tangos. But he came up fighting and did it with so much grace and finesse, the baddies a few feet away didn't even know it happened."

She covered her mouth and shook her head. "That guy... he's something else."

He'd worried about Kid more than once. Something drove that boy, and it had nothing to do with an adrenaline rush. Ruckus hoped he figured it out before it killed him. "He's a menace and freaking amazing SEAL. A few cuts and scrapes. The rest of them are fine. We got the job done without incident." Of course, he couldn't tell her what the job was, but Dana never pressed him for details. She didn't care what they were doing; she knew all of it was dangerous. She only cared about them making it home in one piece.

"That is all that matters. Job accomplished, everyone safe. I'll take it." She kissed his mouth. "Especially you."

She didn't ask him how much time he had before he was called in again. None of them knew that. They were at Uncle Sam's mercy and damned glad to be doing what they did every day. But loving this woman, that was icing on the cupcake.

When the pounding came from the door downstairs, Ruckus sighed. "You know they can't leave me alone for one friggin' day."

She laughed. "You'd better go open it up or they'll come storming in here like commandos."

They got out of bed, went downstairs, and with a growl, he pulled the door open. "Don't you guys have something better to do?"

They walked in, Kid with Mia, his girl, wrapped around him. The other guys were all solo except Scarecrow, who had a cute brunette on his arm.

"Sorry, LT. It's mandatory we have a drink after we get home. You've had all day with your darlin'." One by one they filed past him, some kissing Dana on the cheek, others picking her up in a bear hug, and Tank swinging her around.

Her phone chimed, and she answered, then smiled. "I don't know. Let me see if he's up for it."

He raised his brow when she covered the phone. "You want to meet my boss? She told me she couldn't wait any longer. Drinks?"

"Drinks sound great," Kid said, and the other guys chimed in.

Ruckus turned toward the stairs, grabbing Dana's hand. "We better get dressed, then," he said.

"You do know that means you put her clothes on, not take them off," Hollywood said.

"Shut up," Ruckus growled.

Hours later, he'd met Sara, and everyone was having a great time. Kid was over near the bar toying with Mia's hair, his eyes on her. There was something off with the way she was looking at Kid, and Ruckus felt his gut tighten. The rest of them were either dancing or hitting on Sara. She wasn't complaining.

Then his gaze went to Dana playing pool with Cowboy, who was quite a shark, but she was holding her own. Just like she had with Salazar, in the steaming jungle of the Gap, every step of the way with him. She was magnificent.

He slipped his hand into his jacket pocket and fingered the small box there. He was going to wait, but now, surrounded by everyone, seemed like the perfect time.

He pushed back his chair and walked to the pool table just as she sunk the eight ball. Cowboy was grinning, but when he saw Ruckus crossing the room, his eyes glittered. He motioned everyone over.

He took her hand as she laid the pool cue down. She was still smiling at having beat Cowboy. "Will you marry me?"

Her breath caught, and that smile on her face faltered. He pulled the box out of his pocket, his fingers not quite steady. She looked down at it then back up at him, her eyes tearing up, his chest filling up with more emotions than he could define, but one he was sure he knew what it was. Love.

She stared at him for an instant longer; then she closed her eyes and came into his arms, holding on to him with a desperate strength. Closing his own eyes, Ruckus roughly turned his face against her neck, locking his arms around her.

"I'll marry you, yes."

He grasped the back of her head. "I love you, Dana," he whispered unevenly.

She clung to him, then drew a deep breath, whispering huskily, "I love you, too, Bowie. So much."

She kissed him, a shiver of sensation washing through him. She was so soft, so lovely, and all his.

Exhaling hard, he caught her face in his hands, then reluctantly lifted his head. Tipping her face up, he gave her another soft, gentling kiss. Then he looked down at her, his gaze very serious. "You're not even going to look at the ring?"

"It's really pretty," Tank said, and everyone chuckled.

It was clear it wasn't the ring she was interested in, but she allowed him their moment as he opened the box. From her expression, he could tell she loved it. He slipped it on, and there was a collective sigh from the men and few women around them.

Kid muscled Ruckus out of the way and took her hand. "Will you marry us, too?"

She smiled softly and said, "That's going to be a passel of wifely duties."

Kid's eyes went sly. "We know better than that. It's just that if you marry our LT, well, figuratively, you marry all of us. So I thought I would ask, make it official."

"You'd better watch your *step*, Kid," Dana said wryly.

Kid's head whipped around to Ruckus, his eyes narrowing. Ruckus could only laugh. Kid needed the humility of knowing that he'd told Dana about his fall.

He turned back to Dana. "I think I have his permission."

She gave Ruckus a bemused look. "Okay, yes, I'm all in.

With all of you." She hugged Kid and kissed him on the cheek, then the rest of them.

After all the accolades and hugging were over, Kid held out his hand. "Pay up, boys." He smirked while all the guys slapped money into his hand.

"Hey, what was that all about?"

Kid, laughed and started backing up. "We bet she'd say no. Kid was the only one who thought she'd say yes to marrying us all."

"He is much too smart for his britches," Scarecrow said.

"Yeah," Cowboy said, eyeing Kid. "Let's take him down a notch."

Kid backed up, "Hey, come on guys," he said as he dashed away. While the bar emptied of his buddies all after Kid, Ruckus pulled Dana against him.

"You're sure you want to deal with those knuckleheads?"

"Oh, yes. I'm no dummy, marry you, marry your team. We're family after all."

He closed his eyes. "I guess women can sometimes have something really smart and profound to say."

"Oh you—" she started.

"Caveman," he finished, covering her mouth. Yeah, he knew how to keep his sassy cupcake quiet and satisfied. Something he was going to perfect for the rest of their life.

* * *

Thank you for reading *Ruckus*!
Reviews are appreciated!

Book 2 in the SEAL Team Alpha series, Kid Chaos, is next. Here's a little bit about it:

Kid's a bit gun shy getting involved again when he'd just had his heart torn out. After months of struggling with his break-up of another babe who doesn't understand him, he goes on leave. A vacation is just what he needs until the American beauty from Going Down Tours in Bolivia catches his eye. Kid is there for a couple of weeks to take in the diverse biking adventures offered by the company. Except this babe isn't exactly what she seems, and Kid finds himself in her bed and body before he realizes what kind of danger he's just gotten himself into, not including falling for his sexy guide.

Paige Sinclair is undercover for NCIS and she has no time to get caught up in the cutest, hottest guy she's ever seen walk into the tour company's office. Before she knows what she's doing, she's giving into all those naughty, sweaty, can't-get-them-out-of-her-mind fantasies with him. When things go south with her mission, she's dragging him into her professional life and dealing with a fully capable Navy SEAL to boot. When all the dust settles, will this turn out to be just a fling....or something much more?

GLOSSARY

- Comm - The equipment that SEALs use to communicate with each other in the field.
- DZ - Drop zone, the targeted area for parachutists.
- HALO - High altitude, low opening jump from an aircraft.
- Klicks - Shortened word for kilometers.
- LRRP - Long-range reconnaissance patrol.
- LT - Nickname for lieutenant.
- LZ - Landing Zone where aircraft can land.
- MRE - Meals, Ready-to-Eat, portable in pouches and packed with calories, these packaged meals are used in the field.
- Tango -Hostile combatants.
- SERE -Stands for survival, evasion, resistance, escape. The principles of avoiding the enemy in the field.
- Six - Military speak for watching a man's back.

ABOUT THE AUTHOR

Zoe Dawson lives in North Carolina, one of the friendliest states in the US. She discovered romance in her teens and has been spinning stories in her head ever since. Her heroes are sexy males with a disregard for danger and whether reluctant, gung-ho, or caught up in the action, show their hearts of gold.

Her imagination runs wild with romances from sensual to scorching including romantic comedy, new adult, romantic suspense, small town, and urban fantasy. Look below to explore the many avenues to her writing. She believes it's all about the happily ever afters and always will.

Sign up so that you don't miss any new releases from Zoe: Newsletter.

You can find out more about Zoe here:
www.zoedawson.com
zoe@zoedawson.com

OTHER TITLES BY ZOE DAWSON

Romantic Comedy

Going to the Dogs series
Leashed #1, Groomed #2
Hounded #3, Collared #4
Piggy Bank Blues #5, Holding Still #6
Louder Than Words #7 What Matters Most #8

Going to the Dogs Wedding Novellas
Fetched #1, Tangled #2
Handled #3, Captured #4
Novellas (the complete series)

Romantic Suspense

SEAL Team Alpha
Ruckus #1, Kid Chaos #2
Cowboy #3, Tank #4

New Adult

Hope Parish Novels
A Perfect Mess #1, A Perfect Mistake #2
A Perfect Dilemma #3, Resisting Samantha #4

Handling Skylar #5, Sheltering Lawson #6

Hope Parish Novellas

Finally Again #1, Beauty Shot #2

Mark Me #3, Novellas 1-3 (the complete series)

A Perfect Wedding #4, A Perfect Holiday #5

A Perfect Question #6, Novellas 4-6 (the complete series)

Maverick Allstars series

Ramping Up #1

Small Town Romance

Laurel Falls series

Leaving Yesterday #1

Urban Fantasy

The Starbuck Chronicles

AfterLife #1

Erotica

Forbidden Plays series

Playing Rough #1, Hard Pass #2, Illegal Motions #3

Made in the USA
Middletown, DE
27 August 2021